A SPECIAL THANKS

Thank you to my wife Lisa as well as my sons Luke, Mark and Jake. You make every day of my life an adventure and a journey that I would take over and over again.

I would also like to extend my thanks to all of my family and friends whose love and support has made writing and releasing The Stolen Adventure series such a rewarding experience.

And thank you to Lynette Charters Serembe for her artistic vision in creating the cover art and promotional images, as well as Marj Nilsson and Lisa Mottola Hudon for their editorial services.

You Too Can Join the Adventure Like Us on Facebook

www.facebook.com/TheStolenAdventure

D1111257

THE QUEST FOR CURTANA

CONTENTS

THE QUEST FOR CURTANA

Prologue

Luke had a strange feeling that he had been here before, this ancient passageway burrowed beneath the earth. The musty smell, the moist clay like dirt that clung to his jeans, the aging support beams, all triggered some deep hidden memory. He could feel the tunnel closing in on him. Not usually prone to claustrophobia he had to remind himself to breathe. Despite the anxiety that was growing inside of him he pushed forward.

At spots, the ceiling of this old tunnel had collapsed and been re-dug. He squirmed through on his belly; holding his breath as the dirt crumbled from above. Only God knew what was falling in his hair and down the back of his shirt; a spider web clung to his face; an eerie chill shot up the back of his neck. He hoped upon hope that

1

there was no hairy spider to go along with that web. He hoped upon hope that the fragile rotting frame would not collapse and drop tons of smothering dirt on top of him. These thoughts, these fears consumed his overworked mind. At least he had his lantern, a single beam of light guiding the way through the unknown.

When the tunnel opened to an underground room constructed entirely from stone he exhaled a deep sigh of relief. The single beam of light from his lantern lit small sections at a time. There were intricate designs on the floor as well as around and above the doorways, four in all plus the tunnel that brought him here. The room was circular, the ceiling a dome, all of it expertly crafted. Luke knelt down in the center of the room and wiped away the dust on the floor. With each pass of his hand the details of a compass came into view. He gripped the dial at the center and turned, first to the north, then to the east, then to the south and then to the west. Each turn of the dial caused a stone door to shift and open. When the last door popped from its locked position Luke ran over and pushed the heavy stone out of the way. A long steady hiss escaped from the tunnel behind.

That deja vu feeling grew stronger. He shined the lantern into the corridor and followed the beam of light. There were passageways leading off the main path; both to the left and to the right. At each offshoot he stopped, inspected the gateway, and moved on. Somehow he knew these would not lead him to his destination. He continued until he reached the end of the tunnel where there were three doors -- one in front, one to the left and one to the right. Each door had a dial on it, similar to the one he discovered on the floor of the circular room. Luke faced the door to the left and turned the dial right. He faced the opposite door and turned the dial left. He then approached the dial on the last door, the door in the center, and turned it up toward the ceiling. A strange clicking sound echoed throughout the corridor and the floor began to shake. His feet slipped. Desperately he grabbed for the walls but there was nothing to hold on to. His fingers grasped but it was useless, he could not stop the downward slide. His stomach jumped into his throat, worse than the Wicked Wiley roller coaster at Pirate Land. It made him nauseous and he lost his grip on the lamp.

Helplessly he fell into the pitch black abyss. The sudden drop was terrifying. His body slammed against a solid wall. Without warning the shaft changed direction, bending from vertical to horizontal. The unexpected turn contorted and twisted his body. By the time he was expelled from the shaft he was spinning uncontrollably. Finally he slowed to a stop, dazed and confused on a hard stone floor deep inside the earth.

The sudden jolt to his system made recovery difficult, his head dizzy, his body battered. He needed to regain his composure and prepare for whatever might come next but it was dark and his brain wouldn't cooperate. The sound of small feet scurrying in the darkness sent a shiver up his spine. He dragged his unwilling body across the cold stone floor searching with his hands in the dark, unable to stand. Fortunately he found his lantern. It was at the base of the shaft, it seemed to be in one piece. He banged it against his thigh and was rewarded with the sweet relief of light.

He scanned the area, the beam of light guided his view. This room was unlike the first chamber; this floor was laid with smooth, glazed tiles, these walls were squared and this ceiling flat, one of the walls was covered with beautiful, intricate stained glass designs. Luke moved the light around the room, he saw sconces on the walls and ornate chairs fit for a king. But then, a horrifying sight, there, slumped over a table in the center of the room, was a man. From behind, Luke saw the familiar faded leather jacket and blue baseball cap that could only mean one thing. On this table, in this underground chamber deep below the surface of the earth, was the lifeless form of his hero, his Uncle Al. Luke tried to shake him but it was no use, he gave no response no matter how hard he tried. He fought back the tears. The pain welled up within him. He closed his eyes and began to cry.

"Luke, Luke," a voice echoed from somewhere above. Someone else was here. Surely they could help. He tried to open his eyes but he couldn't see, his trusty lantern no longer provided any light. "Luke, Luke," the voice rang out again. He tried to answer but his voice was mute, choked by his tears.

1. Setting the Trap

"We're still missing a piece...the coin."

Abigail's words hung in the air but Janine was unmoved. Her attention was focused intently on not one but two books that lay on the desk before her. Both books were old leather bound editions, their animal skin pages worn from age. Janine was writing very quickly, translating and transcribing from one to the other.

Abigail threw her soft blonde curls away from her beautiful face and repeated, "I said we're still missing a piece," her words were louder this time, with a slight hint of frustration at being ignored.

"I heard you," Janine responded. But she did not lift her head, nor did she stop her writing. "We need more than just the pieces," she inserted, "...we need *them* as well."

"Who?"

"The kids," Janine replied as if it should be obvious. "And we need them in Argentina."

"You know that's not going to happen," Abigail said with a guffaw. "After what you've told her she'll never let her boys go to South America."

Janine laughed. "I wasn't planning on giving her a choice. Besides, we need her as well." She looked up from her work on the desk. Her auburn hair was pulled back tight to her head, away from her attractive yet stern face, a steely look of determination in her sultry green eyes. "Sometimes you have to push someone right to make them go left."

Abigail did not respond. She was confused and the expression on her picture perfect face showed it.

"Don't worry, I have a plan."

"You always do," Abigail laughed. "Can you tell me about it?"

Just then the door to the office burst open and a pretty woman with strawberry blonde hair raced into the room, an open laptop in her hand. "We've got trouble."

"What is it Kerri?" Janine replied calmly.

"Look!" Kerri put the laptop on the desk in front of her older sister.

Janine took a quick glance at the screen. "They're rather persistent aren't they," she said nonchalantly, returning her attention to the books laid out in front of her.

"And they're getting closer," Abigail added.

There were four images on the laptop screen, four separate camera shots; security cameras from around the mansion. The upper right video showed two men, dressed in navy blue Italian suits, sneaking along the outer wall. Each had dark hair, slicked back, pulled tight to his head, tied in a ponytail, determined yet cautious looks on their olive toned faces. The bottom left monitor showed two more men, same hair, same complexion, same designer suits, scaling the southern wall of the complex. The lower right video revealed a black Hummer limo blocking the front gate.

"It's time for us to move," Kerri inserted, panic growing in her voice.

"Just a moment," Janine added, seemingly unfazed by the turn of events. She continued writing in the book, adding a few final notes before putting down her pen. She gathered several loose papers from the desktop, inserted them in the book and closed the cover. She handed it to Abigail, "Make sure this is delivered."

Abigail took the book and stuffed it under her arm. "Are we ready?" She directed Janine's attention to the screen, the men had penetrated the outer wall and were moving closer to the house.

Kerri stepped to the window and peaked through the blinds. "They're crossing the lawn, they'll be here any second. And they're armed."

"Just one more thing." Janine withdrew the top drawer from the desk, turned it over and reinserted it into the slot. A hidden compartment on the side of the desk popped open. Quickly she stepped around and placed the second book inside the compartment, closed the panel and returned to the front of the desk where she withdrew the drawer and returned it to its original position.

Kerri balked, "They're going to find it."

"They won't have time," Janine replied. She picked up the phone, dialed 9-1-1 and left the receiver lying on the desk. "The police will be here in three minutes." Janine then led her sisters out of the office and out into the foyer.

"CRASH!" They all jumped when the window next to the front door shattered and an arm reached through.

Janine pushed her sisters away from the searching arm that came through the broken glass.

She guided her sisters, first Abigail and then Kerri, across the foyer, past the sweeping staircase and down a narrow hallway to the back of the house. Looking back, one man was through the broken window, another right behind him. Abigail led the way to the back of the house, they could see their way out. CRASH, more broken glass and more intruders. A man jumped in front of Abigail. With a quick kick she separated the gun from his hand. She followed with a thrust of her palm into the center of the man's face, blood spurted from his nose and tears blinded his eyes. One final kick to the groin left him on the floor, writhing in pain. There was no time to celebrate. Another man, pistol drawn, blocked their path out the back of the house, the men behind them closing in.

"In there," Janine instructed, pushing her sisters through a swinging door, away from the intruders and into the kitchen. Inside, Janine wedged a table and several chairs in front of the door, creating a temporary barrier, slowing their pursuers who were already slamming against the door trying to get in. A gunshot rang out, the bullet sizzled through the kitchen door, just missing Janine and lodging into the opposite wall. Kerri and Abigail ducked for cover. Several more gunshots followed, showering the kitchen with bullets and shattered wood. The men rammed their bodies into the door, the tables and chairs held but only barely. An arm reached through the gap, swiping at the impediment, trying to remove the obstacle. On the back of the hand a tattoo, an image of two winged dragons covered by multiple versions of the fleur-de-lis.

Janine turned and raced to the interior wall. She opened the refrigerator door and pressed a button on the outside frame. The inside compartment pivoted into the wall revealing a secret passageway. Kerri and Abigail crawled across the room to their sister and their path to safety. Another ramming of the kitchen door and the table gave way, pieces of broken table and shattered door sailed through the air.

Janine pushed her sisters through the opening and closed the refrigerator door behind them just as the armed men crashed through what remained of the barrier. They entered the now empty kitchen.

Inside the passageway the three sisters huddled in silence. They could hear the men on the other side. "Where did they go? They were just here."

Janine grabbed a flashlight from a shelf on the wall. She turned it on and led her sisters down a narrow stone stairway. The sound of police sirens was the last thing they heard before they raced down the stairway and into the underground tunnel below.

2. The Morning After

Luke was shaken by the image in his dream. It was so lifelike, the feelings so real. But Uncle Al had been here just last night, the ending of the most incredible day of his life.

It was hard to believe how much had happened. Billy and Lynn being kidnapped, rescuing them and escaping from the men with the gruesome sword tattoos, that pointy face Walrus and his gargantuan sidekick No Neck. Getting captured again and finding out that Uncle Al's wife, Aunt Janine, was still alive. And the clock, the mysterious clock with the magical pieces. So much had happened in such a short period of time, now Luke, his brother Tommy and his cousin Katie were in the middle of a strange adventure. No one could predict what would happen next.

It was afternoon now. As quickly as he came, Uncle Al was gone. The excitement of the previous evening and the conversations that lasted into the wee hours of the morning had really taken their toll. Luke, Tommy and Katie were exhausted.

Tommy took Uncle Al's departure the hardest. The previous night was awesome. If he had his way, Tommy would have chosen for it to never end.

Except for three pieces of paper, you might never have known Uncle Al had been there. Each was neatly folded and they were addressed to Luke, Tommy and Katie. Inside they all said the same thing, "Enjoy The Journey."

Mom and Dad were as surprised as everyone else that Uncle Al had arrived in the middle of the night. They spent the morning with him while the kids slept. Dad was disappointed that his brother couldn't stay longer, but like every other visit from Uncle Al, this one ended too soon and left everyone wondering when or if the next visit would come.

All day Tommy moped around the house dejectedly. Luke sat at the kitchen table picking at the food that he couldn't bring himself to eat. Katie on the other hand studied the notes with great fervor. Over and over again she read the single line, passing the pages as if by some magic, the words would change or some hidden meaning would come to the surface. The phrase rang in her head, "Enjoy The Journey."

Katie pulled Luke and Tommy aside. "We need to go back to the house," she whispered to them, carefully looking over her shoulder so as not to be detected.

"What house?" Tommy asked.

"I was thinking the mansion, but maybe we should check both places," Katie said.

"I'm not going back there!" Tommy answered.

"I think she's right," Luke added, adjusting the glasses that had slipped down his nose and beginning to stare off into space just like he always did when he was deep in thought. "There's more to this mystery; I just know it. I bet if we double back to the mansion we can find clues."

"That's what I was thinking," Katie agreed.

"And what about Aunt Janine and her crew?" Tommy asked, trying to bring some sense to the conversation.

"We'll have to be more careful," Luke responded, his mind racing to develop a plan for their next mission.

"Careful?" Tommy asked incredulously. "I think we got off lucky last time. I don't think we'll be that lucky again."

"You may be right," Katie cut in. "So this time we'll have to take special precaution."

Luke made an effort to calm Tommy down. "It will be different this time," he assured him. "It wouldn't have been so bad if we didn't have Billy and Lynn with us."

Tommy knew that they would be in better shape if they didn't have to worry about Billy and Lynn, but this didn't make him feel any better. He thought if either Katie or Luke would take a moment to think this through, they would surely come to their senses. But they were encouraging each other, and whenever Luke and Katie agreed, it usually meant trouble for Tommy. He did convince them to wait until the morning to start the mission, which he hoped would provide enough time to get them to change their plans.

Luke set to work devising a plan to get them back to the mansion. He jotted notes and pulled up files on the Internet. Meanwhile, Katie was putting together a list of items they would need. She started by writing every possible scenario and what she would need for that circumstance, but after much deliberation decided to just create a list of things that would be good to have. Tommy moved about the house gathering the items on Katie's list.

He was simultaneously avoiding Mom and Dad's suspicion and thinking of a solid reason not to proceed with this insane plan.

3. On The River Again

Mom and Dad were stunned when Luke, Tommy and Katie greeted them in bed, already dressed for church. "C'mon Mom," Luke insisted. "We want to get to church. We don't want to waste the day away sleeping."

Dad staggered out of bed and banged his foot on the dresser. He struggled to keep his words under his breath. Mom wiped the sandmen from her eyes, ran into the bathroom and splashed cold water on her face. She laughed when she saw the outfit that Luke had put Billy in for church. It was the same outfit he had worn for Easter, but that was six months ago and it was a much tighter fit now.

In short order Mom and Dad were dressed, Mom changed Billy and they all headed out the door to church. The kids bounced excitedly behind them.

"So why exactly are you up so early?" Mom asked as she fought off a yawn.

Luke said, "Now that we're back at school we don't want to waste one minute of the precious weekend."

"I'm glad you're making the most of your time," Mom replied.

Katie and Tommy were impressed with Luke's answer. Little did they know that he had planned this answer, much like he prepared for every scenario that he thought they might encounter. He spent most of the previous day letting his mind run through every possible situation and then creating solutions. He did more of the same throughout church.

When the mass was over they piled back into the car. "You guys were so good, what do you say we take you out to breakfast?" Dad asked.

"No!" Katie, Tommy and Luke all shouted at the same time.

"Ok, Ok," Dad said, taken aback by the energy in their response.

"It's just that we ate before church," Luke explained, "and we have things we want to get done."

Dad looked at Mom who gave him a shrug of the shoulders. "If they don't want to go out for breakfast." Mom then turned to Katie and said, "I thought we might see your Mom and Dad in church this morning."

Katie leaned forward. "Oh, they never go to the early mass. Mom likes to get her beauty sleep." Katie continued talking about all of the special tricks that Aunt Eileen would do to keep her skin smooth and her hair shiny while Luke bobbed impatiently; anxious to get home and on with their mission.

As the car pulled into the driveway Mom inquired, "So what is it that you guys have planned for today?"

Jumping from the car, Luke answered over his shoulder, "We're going to play down by the bridge." He then ran into the house and headed upstairs to get changed from his church clothes. Tommy and Katie were close behind.

In a matter of moments they were back at the front door, each in play clothes and each with a loaded backpack. Out the door and up the street they walked. When they got to the bridge they climbed down the embankment to the water's edge.

The trek upstream would not be easy. The current was too strong to paddle against. They would have to make their way along the banks of the river, banks that were covered by overgrown brush. Luke pulled out a machete he had taken from Dad's tool shed and handed it to Tommy.

The wooden handle felt right in Tommy's hands. There were a lot of things Tommy didn't understand, but solving a problem with his brute strength was something he was very comfortable with. The handle was smooth from years of gripping and swiping, and the blade was always kept sharp thanks to Dad. The blade whipped precisely through branches and leaves with each swing from Tommy's strong arms. The brush cowered from his mighty blows. The trek was long, but Tommy made short work of whatever stood in his way. After an hour of intense labor, sweat dripping from his brow, Tommy stopped for a break.

"Wow," said Katie. "You're like a machine."

Luke laughed. He had always known this about Tommy and in some ways took it for granted. Handing him a canteen he said, "You're doing awesome. I think we're almost there." Pointing to the river up ahead he added, "That looks like the bend where we got into the water."

Katie looked. "How can you tell; all the banks look the same?"

Luke pointed across the river and up the hill where they could just make out the peak of Fireman's Tower above the tree line. "I know we're getting close because of the angle of Fireman's Tower. It's the same angle we saw from the pool shed."

By now Tommy had regained his breath. He stood up with the machete in hand and once again began blazing a path. As he cut through a particularly thick set of bushes, they emerged to find the embankment where Tommy went into the water, narrowly escaping from No Neck.

Together Tommy, Katie and Luke crept along the path until they could see the back wall of the property. It was very tall and seemingly insurmountable.

"It looks a lot taller now!" Katie trembled.

"You have to remember," Luke said, "we were standing on top of the Jeep when we got over the last time."

"So how do we get over this time?" Tommy asked.

Luke looked at the wall, down to the far end and then back to the other end. "I think we need to go around."

Along the wall they crept, making sure to check in front of them and behind them at every step. As they got closer to the front of the property Katie moved forward and peeked around the corner. "What's that?" she exclaimed.

Luke and Tommy stayed hidden and tried to pull Katie back, but it was no use. She was now boldly walking right up to the driveway. By the time Luke and Tommy caught up with her they saw what she saw, a colorful sign with bright balloons tied to it swinging in the wind. It was a realtor's sign that read, "Open House".

"What's this?" Tommy asked. "What's going on?"

"It's a realtor's sign," Katie answered. "They're selling the house."

Luke got a strange smile on his face. "This could be good. An open house has got to be easier to get into than a guarded one."

4. Open House

Tommy and Katie nodded and smiled. Together the threesome made their way up the driveway, past the animal shaped bushes and to the steep steps that led to the front door. There were other people milling about the property, looking at the garage, checking out the landscaping and inspecting the exterior of the house.

Luke pushed open the front door and entered with Katie and Tommy right at his side. The foyer was the same, but the paintings had been removed from the walls. A man in overalls knelt by the window, fixing a broken pane of glass. The door to the office was open and they could see a middle-aged woman with bleach blonde hair and a red blazer speaking with a young couple inside.

When she noticed the three of them, she excused herself from the couple and came out to the foyer.

"Hello children," she said in a fake tone. "You're not alone are you?"

Katie stepped forward, checking out the sweeping staircase and acting like she didn't hear a word the woman had said. In a formal and proper voice Katie burst out, "I told Mummy if she wants me to go to her alma mater then she is going to have to find a suitable home for my ponies." Turning back to the woman Katie added, "You there. Are the barn's arranged for horses?" Not waiting for an answer, she turned and walked up the stairway, giving the woman in the red blazer no choice but to race to catch up. "You are going to show me around I hope?" Katie asked. Without waiting for a response she marched up the stairs.

"Of course," the woman groveled. "This is a wonderful house, I'm sure it will make a perfect home for your horses while you go to school. So where did you say you'd be going to school?"

"Not horses, *ponies*," Katie corrected her, moving up the stairs and down the hall. "Can you show me the master suites? I want to pick my room."

Breaking out of her confused stupor, the realtor hurried to catch up. "Oh I would be happy to show you around," she called after her.

Luke and Tommy took the opportunity to slip into the office, the same room where Luke met Aunt Janine. They were relieved to see that the desk was still there. The young couple was admiring the stained glass light hanging in the center of the room. Luke motioned to Tommy, pointing first to the desk and then to the young couple. Tommy moved next to the couple and began making gurgling sounds that turned into a vomit like gag, a skill he had learned at an early age. The couple looked at him with disgust and bolted from the room.

20

Luke closed the door firmly upon their exit and moved to the front of the desk. "Let's see if we can find any clues." Pulling the center drawer all the way out of the desk, he turned it over and pushed it back in. The side panel popped open just like before. Tommy stuck his hand inside and pulled out an old leather bound book. He began to open it when they heard Katie's booming voice outside the door.

Luke motioned to Tommy, "Quick put it away," and then pulled the desk drawer out and replaced it in its normal position. Tommy tucked the book inside his belt at the small of his back pulling his shirt overtop to hide any bulge.

The door flew open. "What is this I hear about a boy getting sick in my listing?" The woman came at them with crazy eyes.

"I'm fine now," Tommy said. "I must have smelled really strong perfume," he added, backing up from the woman in the red blazer.

She understood his reference and kept a good distance. "I think it would be best if you waited for your parents outside."

Luke and Tommy didn't need to be asked twice. They scurried out of the office and across the foyer. Before opening the huge front door, Luke looked back at Katie who motioned for them to leave. Luke and Tommy raced out the door, down the steep steps and across the lawn to the gate, where they waited for Katie. And they waited. After what seemed like an eternity, Katie emerged from the house holding a large envelope. She bounded down the steps and sauntered over to the gate. Passing the boys out the gate and around the corner of the wall, she held up the envelope and said, "Got it." Luke and Tommy chased after her.

"What did you get?" Luke asked.

Holding up the envelope, she showed Luke and Tommy. "It's the disclosure forms for the house."

"That's brilliant," Luke stated, pulling the papers from the envelope and reading the forms.

"Why is that brilliant?" Tommy asked.

Paging through the forms, Luke responded, "Because it's a great way to find out more about this property and who owns it."

"You think Aunt Janine owns this house?" Tommy asked. "Or were they just using it while it was vacant?"

"At first I wasn't sure," Katie said, "but as I was talking to the realtor she mentioned something that made me think they either own it or know the owners."

"What did she say?"

"She said the owners live in Argentina and that they left to go back there yesterday and asked her to sell the house."

Luke was now deep into the documentation. "This can't be right. It says here that the house is in Uncle Al and Aunt Janine's name and it gives an alternate address in Argentina."

Tommy was stunned. "You mean Uncle Al owns this house?"

"I bet he doesn't even know," Luke responded. "Aunt Janine must have bought it without him knowing."

They all exchanged confused looks. No one said a word as they made their way along the wall and back to the river.

Finally Katie broke the silence. "So did you guys find anything?"

In all the commotion about who owned the property, they had forgotten about the book from the hidden compartment of the desk. Tommy pulled it from under the back of his shirt.

With wide eyes, Katie exclaimed, "What is it?"

"I think we should wait till we get home to open it," Luke said. Katie and Tommy were stunned, but they decided not to argue.

The trip home was easier than getting there. The path that Tommy had cut with his machete made the walk almost as smooth as floating down the river. After twenty minutes they reached the bridge, climbed the hill to the street and headed home.

Inside, Mom had lunch on the table and insisted that they wash their hands and eat a healthy meal before doing anything else. Reluctantly, they agreed.

Despite wanting to know what was in the book, Tommy ate and ate and ate. All of the hard work had made him very hungry. Katie and Luke quickly devoured their sandwiches then picked at their plates, waiting for Tommy to be done so they could excuse themselves from the table. Tommy finally sat back and patted his belly. A burp escaped his lips.

Katie rolled her eyes. "Are you ready?"

Tommy perked up. "Thanks for the great lunch Mom." Running over, he gave Mom a hug and bolted up the stairs. Katie and Luke raced after him.

Tommy jumped on the bed and pulled the book from the back of his belt. Luke plopped down next to him. Quickly, they opened the old book with the leather binding and yellowing pages. Luke read aloud, "Hans Jacobsen."

5. Learning a New Language

It was awesome. They were holding the journal of Hans Jacobsen, the one that had started Uncle Al and Aunt Janine's journey, the book that had led them to so many amazing discoveries. There was only one problem, the book was written in Danish and none of them knew any Danish.

Luke raced out of the room and in less than a minute returned with Dad's laptop. Logging on to the Internet, he did a search for Danish to English translation. As quickly as he hit the enter key a few thousand links popped up for web sites that provided the service. Luke clicked on the first and then down the line. Most of the web sites were for businesses selling translation services.

He continued clicking links until he found a free service that allowed him to type in a phrase and get back a translation. Typing in a few words from the first page of the journal, they received their response.

Luke fanned the pages of the book. "This is going to take a long time, I better get to work."

Tommy was relieved when Luke said he didn't want to go to the other house and that he wanted to stay to translate the journal. He also resisted Katie's persistent attempts to convince him that they should go to the other house while Luke worked. Instead, he removed himself from the room and did what he did best. He went downstairs and spent the next couple of hours practicing his karate punches and kicks on the body dummy in the basement.

Katie tried to look over Luke's shoulder as he worked, but realized that this was not helping, so she decided to visit Dad and see what she could find out.

Knocking gently on the office door she heard, "Come in," from the other side and meekly entered. She made her way over to her uncle's desk.

"Hi Katie," Dad said, looking up from some papers. "What can I do for you?"

Katie stuttered, not sure what to say. "U...U...Uncle John," she said searching for the right words. "What can you tell me about your brother?"

Dad got a soft smile on his face and a gleam in his eye like he always did when he spoke about his younger brother. "Where do I begin?" he asked himself.

"How about with how he and Aunt Janine met?" Katie suggested.

Dad frowned at the thought. "That's probably not where I would start the story, but if that's what you want to know."

25

And so Katie's uncle began telling her the story of how his little brother had met his wife. It wasn't as glamorous as Katie had imagined for two adventure seekers. The way Dad told the story, they met in the most regular of ways.

"It was thirteen years ago and Uncle Al was visiting for Thanksgiving. He joined your Aunt and I when we went to work at a soup kitchen downtown. Your Aunt Lena was about four months pregnant with Luke at the time.

Dad went on with the story. "Janine was one of the volunteers at the kitchen. She and your Aunt Lena struck up a friendship. Janine would put on a show as a psychic fortune teller. Your Aunt loved it. She would soak up every word. It was all for fun, but she did end up being right about a couple of things."

"Like what?" Katie asked.

"Like your aunt and I having three sons," Dad answered, "and that their names would begin with the letters L, T and W." Dad saw the shocked look on Katie's face and cut her off, "I know what you're thinking, but we had already decided on Luke's name and I think your aunt chose the other names to fit the prediction ... a self fulfilling prophecy of sorts."

Katie was hanging on every word. "So what else did she predict?"

"Oh your aunt and Janine would talk about a lot of things; she could tell you better of course, but you wanted to know how Janine and Al met. Well my brother was smitten with Janine from the first moment he saw her. Who could blame him, a beauty who was smart and down to earth."

Katie thought about this; she agreed Janine was smart and attractive, but down to earth? "How was she down to earth?" she asked.

"Any beauty queen you find working at a soup kitchen when she could be jet-setting all over the planet is, by definition, down to earth."

"Oh," Katie responded.

"It was funny," Dad went on, "because Janine didn't take to Al at first. No matter how hard he tried, she wouldn't give him the time of day."

"So what changed her mind?"

"I think it was your Aunt Lena, another odd thing because your aunt would never set Al up with one of her friends after what he did?"

"What did he do?"

"Well ... Al was not one to settle down. When he was ready to move on he would do just that, move on. Well a lot of your aunt's friends would get upset with her when he did that."

"But it was different with Janine?"

"Yeah," Dad said as he reminisced. "When it came time for Al to move on, Janine went with him and the rest is history."

Katie thought for a little bit and then said, "Thanks Uncle John." She gave him a hug and then bounded out of the office.

"Any time," Dad answered and then returned his attention to the papers on his desk.

Out in the hallway Katie closed the door gently behind her and then moved to the kitchen where she found Mom painting a stencil on the wall. "Hi Aunt Lena," Katie said, jumping up on one of the stools at the kitchen counter.

"Hi Katie," Mom answered. Her face and hands were covered in a mixture of paint and sweat.

"I was wondering if I could ask you a question?"

"Sure," Mom replied. She put her brush down and turned to face Katie.

"What did you say to Janine to make her go out with Uncle Al?"

"Wow," Mom said with a quizzical look. "That's not at all what I was expecting you to ask."

"Will you still tell me?" Katie asked.

"Sure I guess." Mom paused to think back to that day thirteen years ago. "I think I said something to the effect that my husband's brother really likes you and I know he's handsome and rugged, but if you go out with him he'll certainly break your heart."

Shocked, Katie replied, "That's what you said to her?"

"Yep," Mom answered with a smirk.

Katie was confused. "And she still went out with him?"

"Yeah." Mom shook her head in disbelief. "Some women are intrigued by the 'bad boy' and some think they can change a man. I don't know which category Janine fell into, but she did change Al. Before you knew it, they were married and traveling the world together. If it weren't for that terrible accident..." Mom's words trailed off and a tear came to her eye.

Katie felt awkward by the moment, but she still had another question she wanted to ask. "Uh... Aunt Lena?"

"Yes dear?" Mom responded, wiping a tear from her eye.

"Was Janine a psychic?"

Mom laughed. "Wherever did you hear that?"

"From Uncle John."

"That was a long time ago and it was all for fun."

"Did she predict that you would have three boys?"

Mom paused. "Well... yes."

"And that their names would begin with L, T and W?" Katie persisted.

"Yes," Mom said with a sigh. "But she already knew that we had chosen the name Luke and maybe that had an effect on why we chose the names Thomas and William."

Katie's inquisitive mind wouldn't let up. "Weren't Tommy and Billy named after their grandfathers?"

"Yes." Mom was getting flustered. "What is this all about?"

Sensing her discomfort, Katie changed the mood. "Oh nothing really. I just wanted to get to know more about the woman who married Uncle Al."

Mom picked up her paint brush. "If there isn't anything else, I really need to get this done."

Katie had one more thing she wanted to know, but wasn't sure if she should ask. After a moment she decided to inquire. "There is just one more thing. Did she make any other predictions?"

Mom put the paintbrush down again. "That was a long time ago. We talked about a lot of things; I don't remember them all." Mom stopped and stared off into space just like Luke did when he was deep in thought.

"Well if there's anything you can think of let me know," Katie said. She then jumped down from the stool, crossed the kitchen floor and ran up the stairs to Luke's room.

Luke was still hard at work translating the text.

"So how's it going?" Katie asked, sprawling out on the bed next to him.

Luke responded with a grunt, "I made it through several pages, but I'm not even close to being finished."

"My Dad is going to be here soon to take me home. It's a bummer we have to go back to school tomorrow."

"I know," Luke agreed. "I plan on going to the library to see if I can get a book on Danish to English translation, that way I can work on translating the journal at school and on the bus. Can you come over after school tomorrow so we can work on this together?"

"You bet," Katie responded. "By the way, did you know how your Uncle Al and Aunt Janine met?"

"At some soup kitchen," Luke replied, not taking his eyes from the computer screen.

Katie was disappointed that Luke already knew. "And did you know about the psychic predictions?"

"What psychic predictions?" Luke asked, picking his head up to look at Katie.

Just then the doorbell rang. "Oh. That's my Dad, I'll tell you all about it when I come over tomorrow."

Katie gave Luke a playful punch on the shoulder and said, "See you tomorrow." She then jumped off the bed and raced out of the room. Luke tried to call after her, but she was already down the steps. Mom was talking with Uncle Brian in the living room. Katie greeted her father with a big hug and said, "Thank you Aunt Lena, I had a wonderful time. Luke asked me to come over tomorrow, so I'll see you after school."

Luke got down the steps at the same time that Dad emerged from his office, just in time to see Katie and Uncle Brian go out the door and get in their car. They all watched as the car backed out of the driveway.

Once Uncle Brian and Katie were out of sight Mom turned to Dad, "Did you talk with Katie this afternoon?"

"Yeah," Dad replied. "She came in to my office and asked me about my brother."

A concerned look crossed Mom's face. "I think we need to talk." With a furtive glance toward Luke she added, "Alone." She then motioned towards Dad's office.

Luke watched curiously as his parents slipped back to Dad's office. What could be so important they couldn't talk about it in from of him?

6. Help On The Way

The next day was the longest day of school ever. Luke did manage to find a Danish to English translation dictionary in the library, but that made him even more impatient to get home and get to work on the journal. By the time he and Tommy got on the bus to go home, he was ready to burst with excitement.

Luke pulled out the dictionary and started to memorize common words. He figured the more words he knew by heart the easier the translation would be. The raucous activity on the bus made it difficult to concentrate and the slow pace of progress was very frustrating. When Uncle Al had said that Aunt Janine was good at research, Luke thought that it was easy. Look up what you want to know and you're done. But what research really means is spending countless hours studying the same subject and only very rarely finding something special. Luke was beginning to feel that way about Danish, and he had only been at it for one day.

The bus turned down their road, crossed the old steel bridge and stopped in front of their house. Luke and Tommy jumped off. There wasn't as much excitement coming home on a Monday. They waved to their friends and then took their time going down the driveway.

"I'll race you," Luke said, giving Tommy a push and heading for the front door. Tommy barely budged from the push, but it did give Luke a head start to the house.

"That's not fair," Tommy shouted.

Luke was the first in the door and he stopped dead in his tracks. Tommy practically ran him over trying to catch up. The two boys fell in a heap on the living room floor. Luke quickly got up and pointed at the package on the dining room table, a small bundle wrapped in brown paper and tied with string.

Tommy pounced on the package. "It's addressed to us and Katie."

KNOCK! KNOCK! KNOCK! "Anyone home?" Katie called as she opened the door and walked into the house. "Hey guys, how was school?"

"Forget about school," Luke exclaimed, "we got a package from Uncle Al!"

Katie joined in the excitement. "What is it?"

"We have to wait for Dad to get home before we can open it," Tommy explained.

"That's when the packages are addressed to Dad," Luke reasoned, "this one is addressed to us." With that he plucked at the strings. "Let's get some scissors."

32

Luke scrambled up the stairs with the package in hand. Katie and Tommy raced to get there first. From the desk drawer Luke pulled a pair of scissors. With three snips he freed a notebook from the wrapper. It was an ordinary college rule notebook but it was stuffed to the gills with extra pieces of paper. On top was a note from Uncle Al. "Thought this would help you on your way."

They all looked at each other in disbelief. So many questions ran through their minds. Did Uncle Al know they had the journal? Was he the one who left it in the desk? Were they really going to go to all those places? Could they become adventure hunters? This was all going so fast. They were just kids, they couldn't be traveling the globe all by themselves. That was ridiculous. But still it was fun to think of all the romance and adventure even if it was only in the form of reading Hans' journal and Uncle Al's notebook.

Luke recognized the handwriting. "There are notes from every place they went," he announced. Pulling some of the loose pages he said, "I don't recognize this other handwriting but I guess it must be Aunt Janine's. They look like translations of the journal." He leafed through the pages. "I think it's the whole thing." Luke grinned from ear to ear.

Tommy stepped forward. "Since you're going to be burying yourself in Uncle Al's notebook would it be ok if I *finally* get to look at Hans' journal?"

"Yeah, yeah," Luke responded, his face buried in the notebook not paying attention to anything else.

Katie picked up the brown wrapper that the notebook came in. "Guys, the postmark for this package is from Saturday. Uncle Al must have mailed this to us right after he left. Why didn't he just leave it? Why do you think he mailed it?"

Luke gave this some thought. "Maybe he didn't have it on him at the time or maybe he decided later that we might need it."

"You know," Katie said as she thought about it, "he mailed this before we found the journal. At that time he couldn't have known that we would find it."

"Maybe he was covering his bases," Tommy suggested. "That way we would have the information no matter what."

All three pondered these possibilities then they shifted their attention to the books in front of them. Luke spread out some of the pages on the bed and he and Katie began perusing the documents. Tommy sat down at the desk and started to pour over the journal. Silence filled the room as three brains consumed the material and three imaginations filled in the blanks with wonder and excitement.

For hours they studied until Dad came home from work and Mom called them down to eat. Katie made a quick call home to let her parents know that she would be staying for dinner and they all sat down at the table.

Dad asked how everyone's day was but no one responded. Luke, Tommy and Katie were not sure what to say. Their previous stories about Uncle Al and Aunt Janine were not well received and they could think of nothing else.

"Aren't you going to tell your father about the package you three received today?" Mom asked.

Again Luke, Tommy and Katie sat dumfounded.

Mom directed her next words to Dad, "They received another shipment from your brother but this one was addressed to the three of them. I didn't get to see what was inside."

Dad gave them an inquiring look, they began to squirm, "So my brother has brought you into his world of mystery and adventure?"

Luke cut in excitedly, "It's his notebook, all the records from his adventures, every detail of every discovery. It's awesome."

Dad smiled broadly. "Do I get to see it?"

In a flash Luke dashed from the table and up the stairs. He returned moments later with the notebook in hand, minus the loose pages that contained Janine's translations. Handing the book to Dad Luke said, "It's so cool."

Katie strained her neck to see what Dad was seeing. Tommy looked down at his plate sure that this would be the end of their fun. But Dad just paged through the book stopping at various places to take a closer look but otherwise appreciating the unique item, just like he revered everything his little brother sent.

Taking advantage of the pause in the conversation Katie turned to Mom and said, "Aunt Lena, have you thought of any more predictions that Aunt Janine made?"

Mom must have been thinking of something else because her face was pale and she left the table without excusing herself or saying where she was going. Dad put the notebook down and followed her out of the kitchen. From the kitchen table the kids heard Mom say, "It's happening," just before Dad led her back to his office.

When the office door shut, Luke turned sharply to Katie, "What's this about predictions? You mentioned something about that yesterday."

Katie's eyes lit up. "They never told you?"

Luke and Tommy shook their heads.

"Back before either of you were born, when your Uncle Al and Aunt Janine first met, your Aunt Janine was a psychic and she told the future to your Mom."

"Yeah right?!?" Luke said, "No one can see the future."

Tommy cut in defensively, "Luke, they're always telling us about prophets in Sunday school. Maybe Aunt Janine is a prophet?"

Katie rolled her eyes, "I don't know about that, but she did predict that your Mom would have three sons and that your names would begin with the letters L, T and W."

"That can't be," Luke retorted.

"It is," Katie insisted, "you can ask your Mom and Dad, they're the ones who told me."

Luke reached over and grabbed the notebook from in front of Dad's chair. "That's not what I meant," he said, opening the book to a page he had marked and pointing for the others to see. "Right here, Uncle Al keeps referring to L, T and W as necessary elements for the project. I just thought they were scientific symbols or abbreviations."

"I think they are abbreviations," Katie stammered, "for Luke, Thomas and William. Remember how the pieces of the clock each lit up when you guys touched them?"

This revelation, if true, would be classified as one of those moments of research where discoveries are made, when everything comes together to offer greater enlightenment, an epiphany. But when Mom and Dad returned to the table they refused to talk anymore on the subject and insisted that they finish their meals and get busy with their home work.

None of them did a very good job on their homework that night. How could they, with so many other things to think about.

7. The Power of Coincidence

It was a strange week. The days at school were long and slow and the nights were consumed with reading and re-reading Uncle Al's notebook and Aunt Janine's translations. Luke studied through the nights and every spare moment at school. He briefed Tommy about his findings on the bus.

By Friday afternoon Luke finished reading all of the new materials. Together with Tommy he boarded the bus for the ride home, quickly found a seat and began the daily debriefing.

"You know how Uncle Al said that Argentina was their last stop?"

"Yeah…" Tommy replied.

"Well the journal doesn't end there, at least not according to Aunt Janine's notes. If I understand this correctly then the next discovery will be made in Quebec."

"Quebec?" Tommy scoffed, "that's in Canada? How are we going to get to Canada?"

"I don't know," Luke admitted.

The two boys stopped talking and instead stared out the window watching the trees and buildings pass by, their minds deep in thought. They were brought back to the present when the bus lumbered over the old steel bridge and jolted to a stop in front of their house. Much to their surprise Katie stood in the driveway wearing ski goggles and a knit hat.

They jumped from the bus, waved goodbye to their friends and turned to Katie. "What are you doing goofball?" Tommy asked her as he gave her a big hug.

"Kind of warm for that hat isn't it?" Luke teased.

"We're going skiing," Katie announced. "My parents and your parents both won all expense paid trips and we're going to go together." She was glowing as she said it.

Luke tried to dampen her spirit, "It's kind of warm for skiing."

With a punch on the shoulder Katie said, "We're not going now, we're going over the Thanksgiving break."

"I wouldn't get too worked up," Luke said. "That's two months away."

Katie backed away from him and put her hands on her hips, "It's only a month and a half and if I want to get excited then I'll get excited." She then turned her back on Luke and stormed toward the front door.

Luke chased after her trying to apologize. "Fine Katie, I'm excited. Are you happy?"

She turned to him with a huge smile and said, "I'm excited enough for the both of us, you don't have to fake it."

Together Katie, Luke and Tommy walked into the house. Mom greeted them at the door. "I guess Katie told you the good news?"

"We're going skiing over Thanksgiving," Tommy answered.

Luke added a listless, "yeah," his mind still on the journal and the notebook.

"You don't have to look so glum," Mom chided him.

Luke raised his arms above his head in a fake cheer and in a mock tone added, "Yeah skiing," then he led Katie and Tommy up the stairs.

Mom called after him, "You know there is more to do in Quebec than just skiing."

Luke stopped in his tracks and turned to Katie. "We're going to Quebec?"

She nodded her consent.

Luke then grabbed Tommy around the waist and struggled to hoist him into the air. "Yeah," he shouted, "we're going to Quebec!"

From the bottom of the stairs Mom said, "Now that's more like it."

Several weeks passed and early November brought cold winds and early sunsets. Luke, Tommy and Katie were together on a Sunday afternoon making preparations for their trip. Luke had spent the past several weeks studying, researching Quebec and everything about it. He wanted to be prepared for anything that might come their way. He started with maps of the city and the surrounding areas, large maps, small maps and even maps from previous centuries. Cemeteries were also a focus of his study since all the other discoveries had been made in grave related sites. Everything Luke gathered was categorized and filed into a large folder. Every detail he could confirm and many that he was still trying to verify were held in this journal but were also locked in his memory.

Tommy was busy making his own translation of Hans Jacobsen's journal. It was a very slow process but with the use of the Danish-English dictionary he had been able to convert a page a day from Hans' language to something he could understand. The process was made more difficult because he needed to convert all the words and then figure out what each sentence meant. It wasn't as easy as he had expected but he was gaining a certain proficiency in the Danish language.

"Luke, check this out," Tommy said, holding the journal out for Luke to see. "It looks like a page has been cut out."

"I don't think so," Luke replied. "I thought so too but when I compared it to the translation it matched up page for page."

Tommy looked again then said, "Maybe the translation was made after the page was removed?" Holding the journal close to the light he stared closely at the binding. "I'm sure there was an extra page here."

Lying on the floor, reading over a hotel brochure, Katie asked, "Don't you think its too big of a coincidence that our parents win trips to Quebec at the exact moment that we need to get to Quebec?"

When Katie first learned of the last pages of the translation and their corresponding trip to Quebec she was as excited as Tommy and Luke. But as time went on, and as she put the series of events into place, she started to come up with serious questions.

"I don't think it's a coincidence," Luke answered, without lifting his head from his studies, "I think Aunt Janine sent those tickets because she wants us there."

"And we're still going to go?" Katie questioned.

"Well yeah," Luke replied. "We want to go because that's where Uncle Al is leading us. She's just paying for the trip."

Katie was very skeptical, she shook her head in disagreement.

"What are you worried about? Our parents will be with us," Luke reassured her. "She's not going to try anything with our parents there."

"And so will Uncle Al," Tommy chipped in.

"And so will Janine's goons," Katie offered.

"So are you saying we might get to see Abigail?" Tommy asked with a sly smile.

"Ugh," Katie rolled her eyes and turned her back.

Luke moved in to console her. "Listen," he placed his hand on Katie's shoulder, "When the timing is right we're going to tell your parents and our parents all about this. And then we will be one strong team. But for now we need to keep this between us."

"Can't we just tell them now?" Katie pleaded. "This is serious."

"I know it's serious," Luke reasoned. Pulling Tommy next to him he said, "*We* know this is serious, but if we tell them now then they're going to cancel the trip and Aunt Janine and her goons will be coming after us here. Remember what happened with Billy and Lynn?"

Katie did remember everything they went through to get Lynn and Billy back, which was a major reason she was so worried about this trip, or 'trap' as she had begun to label it. But she knew she couldn't convince Luke especially when he had Tommy's full support.

It took a while but finally they agreed that they would tell their parents the moment they checked into the hotel. Katie tried to bring up the subject several more times before they left but that was the last conversation they would have on the subject until the trip.

8. Traveling North

"There's plenty of room for everyone," Dad explained as he showed everyone the RV he rented for the trip. "This way we can all be together instead of going up in two cars."

"How much was this?" Mom asked skeptically.

"Don't think about how much it cost," Dad responded, "think about how much we'll save. There's a kitchen so we won't have to go out to eat, and there's enough sleeping room for everyone." He was so giddy his excitement bubbled out of every word.

Mom laughed at the actions of her overgrown boy.

"This is awesome," Uncle Brian said as he loaded all of Aunt Eileen's bags into the storage compartment.

"And the sofa's convert in to sleeper beds," Dad added, trying to convince everyone else to share his enthusiasm.

He didn't need to. Billy and Lynn were already inside playing on the bunk beds and Luke, Tommy and Katie were checking out the living room and the big screen tv.

Mom had that look on her face like she did every time Dad got one of his crazy ideas. "I have to admit, it will be nice all being together."

That was all Dad needed to hear. "This way we can enjoy the trip as much as the time in Quebec," he said as he hopped into the driver's seat and prepared to hit the open road.

"'It's all about the journey,'" he added, quoting Uncle Al's life motto.

Dad took the first driving shift and Mom sat up front to keep him company. Uncle Brian and Aunt Eileen tried to put Billy and Lynn down for naps, but they were too excited to settle down.

Katie pulled Luke and Tommy to the back bedroom to talk. "You know we're already on the road. We could tell them now and we'd still go to Quebec."

Luke took a deep breath trying to calm down. He turned to Katie and said, "We've already been through this!"

Tommy stepped between them and gestured for Luke to back away. Putting an arm around Katie he said, "Katie, we want to tell them as much as you do, but we know our Mom and she'll have this RV turned around so fast our heads will spin. We agreed to tell them as soon as we check into the hotel, so why don't we just stick to the plan."

Katie didn't feel any more at ease, but she also didn't mention it again. In fact, she jumped up in one of the bunks, put her ear buds in her ears and turned on her iPod, blocking out everything and everyone.

Tommy and Luke played card games with Uncle Brian while Aunt Eileen struggled to keep Billy and Lynn from pulling everything out of the kitchen cabinets. After several rounds of gin rummy Uncle Brian switched with Dad and drove while Aunt Eileen sat in front. Dad was so tired from his stint driving that he immediately retired to the main bedroom and fell fast asleep. Tommy sat in the living room, engrossed in a movie.

It took a while but Mom finally got Billy and Lynn to fall asleep. Returning to the kitchen she slid in next to Luke at the table. "So this is exciting isn't it?"

"Yeah," Luke agreed. "How much longer 'til we get there?"

Mom put an arm around him. "It'll probably be another four hours." Together they sat watching the headlights of passing cars go whizzing by. Mom gave Luke's shoulder a gentle squeeze. "You know your Dad and I are very proud of you."

Luke blushed. "Thanks Mom."

"I mean it, you know," she reassured him. "Your Dad had a crazy idea that you were going to badger us to go on a trip, and you haven't, and I think it shows a lot of maturity."

"Where did Dad think I would want to go?" Luke asked.

"Oh… he thought you were going to want to chase in Uncle Al's footsteps," Mom replied. "He thought you would want us to go to Argentina."

Luke choked when Mom said the word. "Why Argentina?" he inquired, but he already knew the answer.

"Because that's where the story stopped isn't it?" Mom said.

Luke was beginning to feel a little guilty about everything he was hiding. "Would it be so bad to go to Argentina?" he questioned.

"I will never let you go to South America," Mom said in a very firm tone.

"That seems kind of extreme, why not?"

"Let's just say that a long time ago someone once told me that my boys would be in grave danger on a visit to South America and I made a promise to myself that I would do anything to keep that from happening."

Luke looked directly at her and bashfully asked, "Was it Aunt Janine who told you?"

"I don't put a lot of stock in such things," Mom answered. "But she was right about a lot and I'm not willing to risk it."

For more than a moment Luke let various thoughts flood his mind. The one thought that kept coming to the front was the guilt that he felt at not being honest with Mom. Finally he decided it was time to tell her the whole story. "Mom I need to tell you something."

"What is it dear?"

"Well…" Luke paused and in that moment Aunt Eileen called from the front of the RV.

Mom patted Luke on the knee and stood up. "Hold that thought; I've got to see what's going on." Mom moved up front and Luke looked out the window trying to figure out the words to tell Mom what was going on.

Tommy joined him at the table. "How much longer 'til we get there?" he asked.

"Couple hours," Luke answered, avoiding Tommy's look. Instead, he searched outside for signs or landmarks that would give a clue as to their current location.

Tommy pulled a box of cereal from the cabinet, poured himself a bowl and sat down. Mom returned to the kitchen. "Hey Tommy, how was your movie?"

Tommy raised his shoulders and provided an, "Eh," with a mouth full of cereal.

"That good huh?" Mom laughed. Turning to Luke she asked, "So what was it you wanted to talk about?"

Luke looked at Mom, then at Tommy, and then back to Mom. "It wasn't that important; it can wait."

The rest of the trip Luke looked for an opportunity to be alone with Mom, but it didn't happen. There was always someone there to make it impossible to reveal the whole story. Luke figured it didn't make that much difference since in just a few short hours they would be arriving in Quebec and they would be telling Mom and everyone else anyway.

Everyone was thrilled when they finally arrived at the hotel. And what a beautiful hotel it was. A doorman, dressed in a fancy uniform with bright gold buttons down his chest and tassels hanging from his shoulders, welcomed them through tall glass doors into the plush lobby. Large cushioned chairs were arranged in neat sitting areas with colorful fresh cut flowers on every table. In the center of the lobby three glass elevators shuttled guests up and down while providing magnificent views of the city outside. All the while, uniformed bell hops zipped along pushing dollies loaded to the brink with luggage from around the world.

"There's the check-in," Dad said to Uncle Brian as the two of them made a beeline for the front desk.

"This is incredible," Luke, Tommy and Katie marveled as they checked out the surroundings.

Just beyond the registration desk, two escalators led people to a ballroom on the second floor. In between these escalators was the largest aquarium any of them had ever seen. Countless varieties of fish swam inside. Around the edges of the tank a beautifully manicured tropical garden completed the setting.

Billy and Lynn, who had slept for a good portion of the ride, were full of energy. They managed to slip away from the group and grabbed a bellhop's dolly. Giving a push and jumping on, they silently rolled away from the others. The cart continued to pick up speed until it crashed into the wall near the bottom of the escalator. Billy and Lynn landed in a pile, laughing and giggling.

Lynn pointed to the fish tank and Billy knew what she wanted to do, so he led her to a nearby garden. From here they had access to the escalator leading to the second floor. Billy knelt down and let Lynn step on his back. She climbed onto the outside railing of the escalator. Billy followed and soon they were both climbing the railing until they were perched directly above the fish tank.

After a short while Mom and Aunt Eileen noticed that Billy and Lynn were gone and began a frantic search. They looked everywhere for the meddlesome pair. Mom spotted them across the lobby, she kicked off her shoes and darted through the garden. Like a trapeze artist, she launched herself over the plants, landed lightly on the railing and then scurried along the edge.

If they had been given a little more time, Billy and Lynn certainly would have ended up swimming alongside the fish, but Mom got there just in time, grabbing them before they could get into the water. She lowered Lynn down to an awaiting Aunt Eileen and then did the same with Billy. Then she eased herself down from the ledge, acting as if nothing unusual had just happened. Luke and

Tommy exchanged a knowing smile while Katie stared in admiration.

"You know better than that!" Aunt Eileen scolded Billy and Lynn, "Do you know what would have happened if you fell in there?" She was so angry her face turned purple.

The fury in her voice was so intimidating Billy and Lynn were actually humbled into silence, at least until Dad and Uncle Brian finished checking in.

Katie should have been suspicious when she saw the three beautiful clerks behind the counter, but her vantage point did not provide her a view of their ankles or more specifically the tattoos on their ankles. It wasn't until the two pretty bellhops ushered all of them into the elevator that she realized how much danger they were in.

Tapping Luke on the shoulder, she whispered, "Check out the tattoos."

Luke's thoughts were a thousand miles away and he couldn't be bothered with such details. Katie redirected her efforts toward Tommy, but by the petrified look on his face, she could tell that he already knew.

Realizing she would have to act fast, Katie slid next to her father. Surely the Sensei of the leading karate dojo in the tri-state area could handle a couple of petite female bellhops. But it was too late. As Katie pulled at her dad's jacket, she witnessed both bellhops lift masks to their faces. In an instant, the elevator was filled with some strange gas. Katie covered her mouth and nose with her shirt, but that only delayed the effects long enough to allow her to watch all of her family members drop to the floor before she lost consciousness.

9. Bringing Everyone Together

By the time everyone awoke, many hours had passed. They couldn't be sure how much time, but as they would soon find out, it was enough to discreetly move nine unconscious bodies through the streets of Quebec to a private airfield and then onto a private jet headed for Buenos Aires. Now they were locked in a secure room with no windows and only one light.

The room was bare except for nine stunned people recovering from the effects of some kind of knockout gas. Mom moved around the room checking on everyone. Dad was the next to arise, followed by Uncle Brian and then Aunt Eileen. They were talking about their predicament when the kids woke up.

"Where are we and what's going on?" Aunt Eileen cried.

"We're going to be fine," Uncle Brian told her as he put an arm around her shoulders.

"How do you know?" she sobbed. "You don't even know where we are."

Dad was at the lone door to the room, examining the multiple locks and hinges. "If we can find something to pry the pins out of these hinges then we could get this door open."

Uncle Brian moved next to him and started working at the hinges with his bare hands, but it was no use.

Katie, Luke and Tommy huddled in a corner talking discreetly.

"I know we're not in our hotel room," Katie said sarcastically, "but I think its time we tell them."

Luke and Tommy slumped their heads. They knew that Katie was right, not only now, but all the times she tried to convince them to tell their parents the whole story.

"So can I tell them now?" she asked smugly.

"I'll do it," Luke said as he stood up and crossed the room to the four adults. "Guys, we have something to tell you."

Uncle Brian and Dad stopped working at the hinges. They turned their attention to Luke and waited for him to continue.

"I won't bother telling about the first night a couple of months ago when Billy and Lynn were kidnapped," Luke started. "You already heard about that."

Aunt Eileen went pale and reached for the wall to steady her balance. "You mean all that was true?"

Luke nodded.

Aunt Eileen fainted. Fortunately, Uncle Brian was there to catch her and lower her gently to the floor. Luke then proceeded to tell them the story, starting with everything Uncle Al had told them about Hans Jacobsen's journal, the clock and the missing pieces, retrieving the

51

journal from the secret compartment in the desk at the mansion, receiving Uncle Al's notebook and Aunt Janine's translations and the coincidental trip to Quebec.

Mom stood in shock with her mouth agape.

Dad had a furrowed brow and looked upon Luke with both concern and disappointment. "Do you still have your Aunt Janine's translations?" he asked.

Sheepishly, Luke pulled the documents from his backpack and handed them to Dad who skipped to the last page and read. Turning back to Luke he asked, "And where is the journal?"

Luke shrugged his shoulders because he didn't have it, but Tommy stepped forward, pulling the journal from his pack and handing it to Dad, who quickly passed it to Mom.

Mom turned to the last couple of pages and began reading. "It says the last item is in Argentina and that all elements must be present to complete the project."

Tommy looked at his mother in astonishment. "You read Danish?"

Luke jumped forward and grabbed the translation from Dad's hand. "That's impossible; it says the last piece is in Quebec." Pointing to a spot on the page he added, "Look, right here."

"Where did you get these notes?" Dad asked him.

"They were with Uncle Al's notebook," Luke admitted. He then pulled the notebook from his pack. Displaying Uncle Al's note on the cover, he handed it to Dad.

"That is my brother's handwriting," Dad confirmed. "But we don't know when or to whom he wrote it."

Just then a rattling came from the door as the deadbolt locks were being opened from the outside. Uncle Brian assumed an attack position at the door and Tommy stood next to his Sensei. The moment the door opened Uncle Brian lunged forward. A beautiful redhead in a blue suit held him at bay, pointing a gun at his midsection. An even prettier blonde woman in a black suit was next to her. She also had a gun. The redhead pulled the trigger and a dart flew at Uncle Brian. He was quick enough to block the projectile with his forearm but whatever was on the tip of the dart was powerful enough to drop him unconscious in an instant. Tommy caught him as he fell, and the others moved in around him to make sure he was ok.

Kerri, the redhead, and Abigail, the beautiful blonde, moved into the room. They cornered the group and held them at bay with their dart guns while two men, one extremely large with a barrel chest and a square head and the other with a small pointy face and a bushy moustache, moved in to place shackles around the adult's wrists and ankles. Aunt Eileen gasped when she saw the gruesome tattoo of the bloody sword on the large man's neck.

"Where are we?" Aunt Eileen asked with a quiver in her voice. "What do you want with us?"

"You'll find out soon enough," Kerri responded, motioning with her gun towards the door. "Now get moving."

The group was directed out of the room and down a dark corridor to an awaiting elevator. No Neck secured the shackles on Uncle Brian, loaded him onto a sturdy industrial cart and then followed the others down the hallway.

The elevator jerked from its position and began to rise. After a couple of minutes it came to a halt and the doors opened to reveal a glass enclosed lobby with a magnificent view of the city, skyscrapers to one side and a beautiful ocean to the other.

"We're not in Quebec anymore," Mom commented as the crew shuttled them down the hallway toward the only door on the floor. It opened before they got to it, almost as if it had anticipated their arrival. Inside was the most extravagant room any of them had ever seen.

The group was forced into the room and directed to sit around a large conference table surrounded by overstuffed brown leather chairs. Floor to ceiling windows provided scenic views in every direction. They could see a sprawling city out one side and the open expanse of ocean on the other.

On the table sat the maze that Uncle Al had given to Luke for his tenth birthday. When no one was looking, Luke leaned forward and touched the fish hook in the middle of the contraption. His touch caused the hook to emit a green glow and the balls to feed automatically through the complex wire path.

The automated toy was mesmerizing, capturing everyone's attention, until a door opened at the far side of the room. The adults thought that the sharply dressed woman with the air of sophistication who came out was the leader, but the children knew this was only Heather, Aunt Janine's assistant. She approached the table and surveyed the group, taking special note of the cuffs on the adult's wrists. She then motioned toward Tommy and said, "Shouldn't his hands be shackled as well? I know the trouble he has given you in the past."

Tommy grinned, but his smile quickly faded when No Neck approached and placed handcuffs on his arms. Mom was mortified when she saw her son treated this way. Dad's face turned purple with rage. At this point everyone was so consumed with either the maze on the table or the events between Tommy and No Neck that no one noticed Aunt Janine emerge from the adjacent room. She approached the table.

"Long time no see Lena," Janine said to Mom as she bent over and kissed her gently on the head.

Mom was speechless. She stared at Janine in utter disbelief. The whole story was beginning to take shape, but it did not become reality until she saw Janine, the woman she presumed dead, alive in the flesh. "You really are alive," Mom gasped.

Janine scoffed, "You can't believe everything your brother-in-law tells you."

Luke was enraged when he heard Janine say this. He stood to object, but was quickly forced back into his seat by the Walrus standing behind him.

Janine then moved to the far end of the table where Aunt Eileen was caring for Uncle Brian who was still motionless on the cart. "I don't believe we've met, I'm Janine."

Aunt Eileen looked at her with scorn and contempt. With more courage than anyone thought she had, Aunt Eileen turned on Janine and said, "So you are the one responsible for kidnapping my daughters and dragging all of us to some unknown place?"

"I assure you, your daughters and nephews were never in any real harm," Janine explained. "I need them. And as for this place, I'm sure your friends here know where we are."

All eyes turned to Mom, who bent her head down and said aloud, "South America."

Janine then directed everyone's attention to Luke who added, "Argentina."

Finally Janine moved next to Dad who finished with, "Buenos Aires."

With a wink to Aunt Eileen, Janine said, "It looks like you knew a lot more about this place than you thought."

Aunt Eileen was shocked, perhaps by the predicament she now found herself in, but more likely because Mom and Dad knew as much as they did without telling her.   Regardless of the reason, she was not comforted by this revelation.

Janine just offered a condescending smile.   She reveled in being in a position of dominance and was savoring every moment.   Moving around the table, Janine stopped behind Mom and placed her hands on her shoulders.   "Do you want to tell everyone why we're here?"

"To fulfill your prediction," Mom responded sullenly.

"Not my prediction," Janine laughed.   "No, this is about Soren Jacobsen's prophecy.   I'm just making sure it all happens for my benefit."

Luke looked around the table, first at Katie and Tommy, and then to Mom and Dad, trying to catch someone's attention.   Noticing his secretive efforts, Janine approached him.   "Haven't figured it all out yet have you?" He shook his head.

Janine continued.   "It all started about fifteen years ago when I found Hans' journal," she explained.   "It was fascinating, every detail was there, even things I never could have imagined.   It took me over a year to get all the translations right and confirm the research.   It took a while, but eventually I figured out that I would need your mother and her sons if I was going to succeed.   How shocked was I when I finally found the heir to the Jacobsen prophecy and realized I was twelve years too early."

"You knew before we met?" Mom questioned.

"Before we met?" Janine said with a guffaw.   "If it weren't for the journal we never would have met."   She turned to Heather and added, "Like I would have been working in some random soup kitchen."   Returning her attention to Mom she said, "I positioned myself there specifically so we could meet."

"And all those psychic readings?" Mom inquired.

"Oh they were real," Janine continued, "but they weren't mine, they came from Soren by way of Hans' journal. I told them to you in order to gain your trust. The more you believed me the more I shared with you."

Mom had a look of betrayal on her face. "And your relationship with Al?"

"Albert?" Janine grinned. "When he started flirting with me I was repulsed. All this, 'It's all about the journey.' When I found out he was your brother-in-law I figured what better way to stay close to you. But then Albert wanted to head off to all parts of the world, so I came up with the plan to let *him* find the journal. He was amazed at how quickly I was able to decipher it. I shared just about everything with him, everything except for a couple of key pages that connected the journal with you."

Tommy shot a glance at Luke and mouthed the words, "The missing pages."

Janine pulled a remote control from her pocket, and with a flick of her wrist, curtains slid on their rails to cover the windows and a screen lowered along one wall. Another click on the remote and a projector rose up from the center of the table and an image was displayed on the screen. It was the Jacobsen family tree, starting with Soren and working its way down. Janine used a pointer to show where the diagram led to Mom's family and the initials for her three sons.

"By now you know all about Soren Jacobsen's inventions," Janine said, pointing to the maze on the table. "Each one is matched up with one of you," she added, directing a pointed finger at Luke then Tommy then Billy. "And of course you too," she said to Mom. "Which is why all of you are here. According to the journal I need all of the pieces, along with their human match, in order to realize the true power of the clock."

"So why are we here?" Aunt Eileen quipped.

57

Rolling her eyes Janine responded, "Because it's hard to get good help these days. You were supposed to be left in Quebec, but when you passed out they didn't know who was who, so they brought all of you here." Circling around the table to the cart where Uncle Brian was lying, she gave him a kick and added, "It might just work out for the best since this one appears in the journal as well." Redirecting everyone's attention to the screen, Janine pointed to the chart where Uncle Brian's name appeared with the letters K and L beneath it.

"So why did you send us to Quebec?" Luke asked.

"It was necessary," Janine explained. "I needed you in Argentina and I knew your mother would never let you come to South America. So we devised a plan to capture you in my hotel in Quebec and fly you here. In Canada, if you know the right people and pay the right price, you can get anything, or anyone, through customs." With a sneer she added, "All we had to do was send you a package making it look like one from dear Albert. Then tickets from a phantom prize contest and voila, you came to us."

Dad interrupted her gloating, "So what do you plan on doing with us now?"

With a broad smile Janine stated, "I think it's time we go on a little field trip."

10. A Meeting with Destiny

The shackles around the ankles of Mom, Dad, Aunt Eileen, and Uncle Brian were removed, but the handcuffs remained on their wrists. From the penthouse, everyone was led into a large service elevator and they descended to the hotel's underground garage. There, waiting for them, was an old white school bus.

Sitting in the driver's seat was an old man with leathery skin and a scruffy beard. He looked like a native Argentinian. An unfiltered cigarette dangled from his dried lips and a Yankees baseball cap covered his head. On either side of the bus door were two women in their mid twenties wearing identical green fatigues and toting automatic rifles. Unlike the other members of Aunt Janine's crew, these women were much more muscular and not nearly as attractive.

When Aunt Eileen shuttled onto the bus, she tried to signal the bus driver, "We've been kidnapped you have to help us!"

Either he didn't understand or he had no interest in helping. Either way, the entire group was loaded into the vehicle.

Mom, Dad, Uncle Brian and Aunt Eileen were separated and forced to sit with blindfolds on and surrounded by different members of the crew. The women in green sat behind Uncle Brian. No Neck and the Walrus sat behind Dad. Heather and Abigail surrounded Aunt Eileen. Kerri was near Mom. The children were forced to the back of the bus while Aunt Janine sat next to the bus driver, giving directions.

The bus pulled out of the garage, drove through a few crowded city streets and then out into the vast expanse of open country roads. The ride was very quiet except for the rattle of the old bus as it bounced along the pothole strewn road. Anytime any of the adults would try to talk they were immediately silenced. Every once in a while Luke, Katie and Tommy managed to exchange quiet communications without anyone noticing. Billy and Lynn sat in a seat by themselves, stunned into silence by everything that was happening.

Luke had a feeling that he knew exactly where they were going. He imagined Uncle Al making this same trip with Aunt Janine, No Neck and Abigail. He tried to soak in every detail along the way, to remember everything he could about the journey to discover the secrets of Soren Jacobsen's creations. As his mind got lost in the intrigue and adventure, it was easy to forget the imminent peril that lay before them.

For miles the bus trudged through bumpy country roads, passing an occasional hut or store. After about an hour the landscape changed from open land to dense forest.

The country road turned into a winding mountain path more fit for a braying animal than a modern day vehicle. Luke tried to remember every turn, however, no recognizable landmarks were evident and every road looked the same. The bus continued to climb and at times seemed to struggle with the steep slope and the weight of its passengers. As they reached the summit of a particularly steep hill, they saw an open lot with a small stone building situated in the middle. On top of the building was a bell tower and on top of that a wooden cross, worn from years of rain and harsh winds.

"This must be the place." Luke said aloud, but he was silenced by a stern look from one of the women in green.

Sure enough, the bus came to a halt and all passengers were led off.

Outside, No Neck removed the blindfolds from Mom, Dad, Uncle Brian and Aunt Eileen, but kept the cuffs in place. He then took a large bag of sand from the bus and dropped it onto Uncle Brian's shoulders, forcing him to carry it.

They didn't go to the church as some may have expected. Instead, Janine led them down the hill to an adjoining cemetery. The lot was surrounded by a low stone wall, deteriorating from the elements and age, at the center of the wall was a small wrought iron gate that was falling from its hinges. From the look of it no one had spent any time here in years. Janine approached the gate, kicked it open and forged a path between the headstones.

When Luke, Tommy and Katie passed through, they immediately began checking out head stones, looking for any names they knew. They saw memorials of all shapes and sizes. Years of rain and wind had eroded most of the engravings, leaving them virtually unreadable.

After a short walk, they reached an area that had no more head stones, only overgrown brush, Janine motioned to one of the women in green, "We need a path right here."

The woman pulled a large blade from her belt and slashed a rough path through the thicket. Everyone followed in single file until they reached an opening in the bush. In this clearing there were eight headstones, arranged in a square facing inward, one headstone at each corner and one along each side.

Janine directed Abigail and No Neck, "Take your positions on the two eastern corners," she said to them.

They moved to the headstones on the east side corners of the square. Janine crossed to the headstone in the middle of the opposite side.

"Wait for my signal and then push down on your tombstones." Janine leaned on top of the stone, using all of her weight to push it down. It shifted several inches.

Upon Janine's signal, No Neck pushed down on his headstone and Abigail did the same on hers. Everyone stared in awe as the headstone between No Neck and Abigail began to move all on its own.

"Take the sandbag and put it here," Janine instructed the red haired woman.

Kerri did as she was told, sliding over to Uncle Brian, taking the bag of sand from his shoulders and placing it on top of the tombstone near Janine. The weight of the sand kept it held down.

Janine walked over to the headstone between No Neck and Abigail, the one that had moved on its own, and with one hand pushed it aside revealing a passageway deep into the cold earth.

Flashlights were handed out to Janine and the rest of her crew. The Walrus unlocked Mom's handcuffs. He did the same for Dad, Aunt Eileen and Tommy. When he got to Uncle Brian he turned to Janine, "What should I do about him?"

"Keep his cuffs on," she responded. Janine then directed her next words to her hired mercenaries, the women in green, "If anyone comes out without us you know what to do."

The two women sat on the headstones on the eastern corners, the same ones that No Neck and Abigail had been holding. With their rifles, they motioned for everyone to enter the hole. No Neck led the way, followed by Luke, Katie, Tommy and then Abigail. Before entering the hole, Luke checked his backpack. His lantern was right where he expected it, but he did not bring it out. Instead, he entered the tunnel, following in the darkness.

Aunt Eileen and Uncle Brian went in with Lynn. Heather followed at a distance, wary of what Uncle Brian might do. Then Mom and Dad entered with Billy. Janine was the last to enter the passageway.

The tunnel was very dark and smelled musty. The walls and floor were hardened dirt and the wood beams that supported the ceiling were noticeably deteriorating. At points, the ceiling had collapsed and the passage was so small that everyone was forced to slither on their bellies -- even Lynn and Billy. The lights from the flashlights did little more than cast eery shadows on the walls. For several hundred feet they crawled until they emerged in an open chamber cut from stone.

As each person emerged from the tunnel Abigail directed them with her flashlight, "Against the wall."

One by one they lined the perimeter of the room. Meanwhile, No Neck pulled a large lantern from his pack and placed it on the floor in the center of the chamber. By the time Janine came through, everyone was in place and the collection of lamps cast a yellow orange glow throughout the room.

Luke noticed the arc of the ceiling. It was a finely crafted dome. As his eyes adjusted to the light he also recognized that there were five exits, the tunnel they had used to get here plus four more portals that were sealed shut. Luke wondered how these would be opened and which door Uncle Al had chosen when he was here.

Tommy began to nudge Luke with his elbow and then directed his attention to the doors, and more importantly, the writings in strange script on the wall above each. Luke had no idea what they meant until Tommy whispered, "They're messages from Soren."

Luke wanted to know how Tommy knew this, but he didn't have time to ask, Janine was down on her knees in the center of the room, wiping away dirt from an insignia marked on the floor. She took a deep breath and blew the remaining dust from the spot, revealing a detailed mariner's compass. Gripping the dial of the compass she performed a series of turns until the portal to the right popped open.

"Abby," she said, motioning toward the beautiful blonde who began pushing on the door.

A hiss escaped from the gap created by the door moving from its spot. The more Abigail pushed, the wider the gap became until the opening was large enough for even No Neck to get through.

Abigail entered first, shining her flashlight around the newly revealed tunnel. With a push on his back Luke was forced into the tunnel next. From what he could see, this passageway was fashioned from stone. As they walked deeper and deeper into the tunnel Luke noticed more doors, but Abigail did not stop at any of them. Instead, she continued until the tunnel came to a dead end with three doors, one to the right, one to the left and one straight ahead. Each of these doors had a mariner's compass on the front.

Abigail did not wait for the rest of the group, she immediately set to work turning the dial on the left door to face the one in the center and repeating this process with the door on the right. Luke watched intently as she directed her attention to the compass in the center door. This dial she turned straight up toward the ceiling. When the dial clicked into place the stones beneath Luke's feet began to shift, he tried to grab hold, but it was no use and in an instant he was sliding down and down, bouncing this way and that, until he spun to a stop in total darkness.

He couldn't see a thing, it was pitch black, when he stood up his feet were taken out from beneath him by the next person to come down the slide. He crashed to the ground landing on top of Katie, but neither one of them had a chance to get up before Tommy came barreling into them. This process continued with new bodies sliding and crashing in the darkness until a lantern illuminated the area. Soon several lanterns provided ample light to study the surroundings.

This room was unlike the first chamber or the tunnels. It was furnished with a table and six chairs, sconces holding torches were built into the walls and there were windows, five of them. The windows were stained glass, depicting scenes from the bible. The first showed Abraham about to sacrifice his son Isaac, the second showed Noah gathering animals two by two on the ark, the third depicted Moses parting the red sea, the fourth was of Jonah in the belly of the whale and the last was of Jesus Christ on the cross.

Standing in this room gave one the feeling of being in a church. If Luke didn't know any better he would have thought he could just walk outside and go about his normal life. But he did know better and he was both excited at the prospect of what might happen and terrified at the same time.

"Get them in position," Aunt Janine said as she took a seat at the head of the table. The members of her crew quickly guided Luke, Tommy, Billy and Mom to seats around the table. Janine then opened a pouch that was secured around her waist and produced the rod from the tarantula and the cog from the egg scale, which she placed in front of Tommy and Mom respectively. No Neck then placed the maze in front of Luke.

With a hand extended, Janine said to Luke, "I believe you have something for me?"

Luke reached into his backpack, pulled out her translations and handed them to her.

She dropped the stack of papers on the table. "That's not what I'm looking for."

Luke was confused at first, but then he realized what she meant. Rooting deep into his pants pocket he pulled out the coin. Janine's eyes lit up as she took it from him. She admired it briefly before placing it on the table in front of Billy. No sooner had she put it down then Billy grabbed at it, causing the coin to glow. When Janine tried to take it back, it bounced on the floor and rolled away. Several members of Janine's crew shined their lights to the floor and a mad scramble ensued. By the time the dust settled, Kerri held the coin. She walked back to the table and placed it down in front of Billy, this time just out of his reach.

Janine withdrew a notebook from her bag and opened it on the table. It was a translation of Hans Jacobsen's journal, only this version was complete and unaltered.

Luke looked down at the pages, trying to decipher Janine's notes. They were not in English and Luke wasn't sure what language it was.

After a few moments of reading to herself, Janine made a gesture to Heather who took a bag from her shoulder, placed it on the floor and removed the clock. She moved to the table, and slid the clock into a groove in the center of the tabletop. Janine reached into the interior of the clock and touched the ring. It started to glow and emit a soft hum.

Janine motioned to Mom, directing her to a place inside the clock just below the ring. "Insert the cog here." Once Mom had done this, Janine directed Tommy to place the glowing red rod into the hole in the center of Mom's cog. Then Billy, with Mom's assistance, inserted the coin on the other end of the rod. No one made a sound, every eye was transfixed on the events taking place at the center of the table.

"It's your turn," Aunt Janine said to Luke.

As if by instinct, Luke knew what to do. He reached into the center of the maze, causing the unit to glow green and sending balls moving through the wires. With a twist of his wrist he turned the fish hook and the balls stopped moving. When he removed the fish hook, the maze stopped glowing, but the fish hook still held its green aura. Carefully Luke inserted the fish hook into the clock, attaching one end to Mom's cog, and the other to Billy's coin.

As soon as Luke withdrew his hand, Janine snapped at him, "What did you do? Why isn't it working?" She was infuriated beyond belief. At first she stood up and paced the floor, then she went back to her notebook and read. She read the same pages over and over again. She then took the pieces out of the clock and had everyone repeat the process of putting the pieces together. Again, it did not work and again she made everyone do the whole routine over. This went on for a long time until finally Janine threw up her hands in disgust and said, "That's it, we're out of here."

Her crew packed up their bags. The tension in the room was palpable. Heather grabbed the clock from the table and No Neck seized the maze. Janine then led the way back up the slide, Heather and the Walrus were close behind. The remaining members of her crew, Abigail, Kerri and No Neck all followed taking the light from their lanterns with them. Mom then instructed Luke to go next and he scurried up the slide. When he reached the top, he was rudely greeted by No Neck's foot pushing him back down. He couldn't keep from sliding and in the process took out Katie and Tommy who had been right behind him. They all slid back into the room and above they heard the grim sound of the portal being closed.

"What was that?" Aunt Eileen shrieked in the darkness.

Normally Uncle Brian would console her in times of stress, but this time no one said a word. They were trapped and they had no hope of escape.

11. Important Moments in Time

The darkness was frightening and made even worse by the whimpers that began to escape from Lynn and Billy. Aunt Eileen and Mom were holding them, but it was not enough to calm them down.

During his slide into the room, Luke was separated from his backpack and it took him several minutes of blind searching before he was able to put his hands on it. Once he did, it was only seconds before he was able to provide everyone with the sweet relief of light. With lantern in hand, he then helped Tommy and Katie find their packs and soon three lanterns were illuminating the chamber. Billy and Lynn calmed down, but now everyone could see the look on Aunt Eileen's face and the terror in the room began to grow once again.

Dad approached Luke. "What else do you have in your pack?"

Luke handed it to him and held the light so Dad could see. Shuffling through the items, Dad pulled out a paper clip and went over to Uncle Brian. In a matter of seconds Dad picked the lock of Uncle Brian's handcuffs and he was loose. Uncle Brian then took Katie's lantern and made his way up the slide with Dad right behind. They spent a good deal of time trying to open the hatch, but it was no use and finally they gave up and returned.

"The hatch is sealed tight," Dad explained, "but there has to be another way out of here."

He and Uncle Brian searched every spot, looking for a way out, Uncle Brian even grabbed a chair and launched it at one of the stained glass windows. It bounced off the window and fell to the floor, not even causing a scratch.

Mom approached Dad. In a whisper she asked, "What are we going to do?" She tried to keep her voice low, but with the combination of the chamber's echo and everyone else's silence, it was clearly audible to all.

"We're going to get out of here," Dad replied confidently, but the look on his face said otherwise.

Mom tried to change the mood in the room, "So why do you think the clock didn't work?"

Tommy was quick to respond, "Because she didn't have all the pieces."

"What do you mean?"

"The cross," Tommy stated. "Aunt Janine must not know about Uncle Al's cross."

"What cross?" Mom asked.

"There's one more piece to the clock and Uncle Al has it. It's a cross that glows blue when Uncle Al touches it."

Mom thought about this for a moment then turned to Tommy. "Do you still have the journal?"

Tommy rifled through his pack, pulled out Hans Jacobsen's journal and handed it to Mom. She flipped through the pages. Soon she found what she was looking for and began reading. "It says here that when the five pieces are brought together then the clock will unlock the greatest power to the person who controls it. So there were only five pieces."

Luke, who had remained silent during the discussion said, "The ring is part of the clock; it's not one of the pieces. The five pieces are the rod, the cog, the coin, the fish hook and the cross."

Mom looked at him in wonder. "How can you be so sure?"

He smiled and pointed his flashlight at one of the stained glass windows, the one of Moses parting the sea. Approaching the window he pointed to a spot on Moses' staff that was the exact size and shape of the rod from Tommy's tarantula. "See the rod?"

Skepticism filled the room, but before they could voice their views Luke moved to the next window and pointed to an image of Mom's cog on Noah's ark. "Look at Noah's Ark; see the cog?" Moving to the window of Jonah and the whale he pointed to Jonah's clothing, "see the fish hook?" It blended into Jonah's clothing but it was there. "And here," he added, pointing to the window of Abraham and Isaac, "it's Billy's coin."

By this time he didn't need to convince anyone, but he moved to the window of Jesus Christ and sure enough on Jesus' hand was an image of the cross, exactly as they had remembered it on Uncle Al's necklace.

Everyone was stunned.

"How did you notice that?" Mom asked.

"I don't know," Luke responded. "Those images just jumped out at me."

The excitement of the discovery had lightened the mood, however it was short lived. Soon the reality of their predicament returned, and the eerie silence came with it.

The chamber became a very somber place. Everyone was in a different stage of coping with this crisis. Billy and Lynn were hungry and began an incessant whining for food. It was draining just listening to them. Aunt Eileen struggled to keep her sobs from becoming a full on crying jag and Uncle Brian paced the room both searching for some way out and releasing pent up energy. Luke and Tommy rifled through their backpacks, searching for something, anything that might help. Dad studied the stained glass windows, wondering why it did not break from the force of the chair.

Mom led Katie to the table and pulled a small tattered notebook from her back pocket. It was old and showed years of wear. "Katie, I know you asked about this before," Mom said. "I was planning on showing you on our trip to Quebec."

Katie took the notebook and opened it. The writing inside was a scrawl of notes from many years ago. It took Katie a while to read Mom's writing in the dim light. The first line read, "You will bear three sons and their destinies will be tied as one." Katie looked at her Aunt Lena and a tear came to her eye.

"I know," Mom consoled her. "Do you still want to know about Janine's predictions?"

Katie nodded, but she wasn't sure she really wanted to know. She returned her eyes to the book and read the second line, "The three sons shall carry the initials L, T and W." The next several predictions had to do with events that happened earlier in the boys' lives. Katie read them and looked at Mom, who only nodded her confirmation.

Continuing through the book, Katie was amazed at the number of prognostications and the accuracy of each. Then she reached the line about their current trip. "Your three sons will travel to a southern land and it will be the location of their greatest adventure and their greatest dread." Katie choked on the words, but couldn't keep herself from reading them over and over again. Tears filled her eyes and she was unable to go on.

Sensing the moment, Mom took the book and put her arm around her niece. They stayed like this for awhile just huddled at the table, not saying a word. Mom glanced down at the book and read the words that caused Katie to break down. She also needed to take a moment to regain her composure. Turning the page, Mom read the last of the predictions. "Oh my, I forgot about that one."

Katie, whose head was leaning on Mom's shoulder asked, "What?"

"Janine's very last prediction," Mom replied and then began reading from her notebook. "In God's hands they move forward." The moment the words escaped her lips she wished she had not said them out loud.

12. Visiting the Museum

The old white bus rumbled down the mountain road, moving slowly and carefully in the darkness with only dim headlights to lead the way. No Neck leaned forward in his seat to speak with the Walrus. "I don't like hurting kids," he whispered. "I was really starting to like the little ones."

Despite his efforts not to be heard, Janine sprang to her feet and stormed back to him. "How many times have I told you, we're not going to hurt them!"

No Neck stammered, but still managed to get the words out of his mouth, "But...but...but we left them there to die."

Janine rolled her eyes. "I've told you, I need them. I need *them* more than I need *you*. We are going to return and when we do, they'll be so relieved to see us they'll finally cooperate."

No Neck's mind was put at ease over the issue, but there was still something he wasn't sure about. Before he had a chance to even ask the question, Janine got right in his face and in a tone meant only for him said, "We're going to the museum in Buenos Aires; they have something that is very important to me." And in a sarcastic drawn out tone she added, "Do ... you ... understand?"

"Oh," No Neck responded. He nodded to confirm his understanding, but he didn't really understand. He was afraid of Janine, despite being twice her size. Maybe it was her crew of female commandos or maybe it was her domineering attitude, but regardless of the reason, he feared her.

The bus continued slowly on its path. It was so dark and the headlights were so ineffective that at times the bus driver had to stop, get out of the bus with a flashlight and check the road ahead. It didn't help that the road was not much more than a trodden path, more appropriate for a mule than a bus. At one point, when the driver stepped off the bus, he was nearly hit by a motorcycle zooming past on its way up the mountain.

The entire crew was relieved to reach the highway and the comfort of paved roads. The pace of travel increased and they reached the city just as the sky was beginning to reflect the first rays of the morning sun.

The museum was large, very large; it covered a city block. They pulled into a back alley behind the building and came to a stop. Everyone departed, except the driver. Janine stayed behind long enough to give him his orders and then joined the rest of the group on the sidewalk.

Janine addressed the women in green. "I need you to guard both ends of the alley, but don't be obvious."

The women left their rifles on the bus, replacing them with 9mm pistols that they secured safely and discreetly inside their belts. Without a word, they moved in opposite directions until they were in position to stand as lookout at either end of the alley.

"You two wait right here," Janine said to No Neck and The Walrus. "Call me with any news."

Janine then led the rest of the crew toward the building and a service entry next to the loading dock. A camera was positioned above the door. Heather, the oldest of Janine's crew, pulled out an envelope from her bag, fanned it open, revealing its contents to the camera, and then turned and placed it under the front end of a nearby dumpster. She exchanged it with another envelope that was already there. A buzzer sounded and the door popped open.

Abigail led the way into the building, racing down the hallway and checking around the corner. "The coast is clear," she called, signaling for Janine, Heather and Kerri to follow. They continued this process deep into the building until they reached a darkened corridor and a set of elevator doors.

Heather pulled something from her pants pocket, showed it to the security camera above the elevator and in an instant the doors opened. The four women climbed in. Without pushing a button, the doors closed and the elevator descended to a level well below the ground where the doors opened and the crew filed out. Once again Abigail led the way.

This hallway was short and ended with two doors. The first read, "Archives," and the second, "Restorations". Heather pulled a key from the envelope she had found beneath the dumpster and opened the door marked "Restorations".

Inside, Janine knew exactly where to go. She moved to a cabinet along the left wall, opened it and withdrew a glass case containing an old leather bound book along with a couple of intricate contraptions. Janine's heart leapt when she laid her eyes upon the objects.

The glass case was laid out on a nearby counter. Janine opened the lid and began paging through the book. Heather and Abigail removed the remaining items from the case and loaded them into their bags.

"We got what we came for," Janine announced, "it's time to get back to the chamber. She closed the book, tucked it under her arm and headed for the door where Kerri was standing guard.

Determined and with purpose they strode down the hallway, back to the elevator. Heather once again held something up to the security camera, but this time there was no response. She held it up again, but still nothing happened. She looked at Janine who gave her a quick nod, prompting her to put down her bag, withdraw another envelope, lift it to the camera, fan it open to reveal the contents and then drop it into a nearby receptacle. The elevator doors sprang open and the crew entered. The elevator took them back to the original floor where they backtracked through the hallways to the rear exit of the building. Once outside, Heather looked for the envelope she had placed under the dumpster, but it was gone. The women jogged back to the alley where No Neck and The Walrus were now standing next to the bus.

"Everything work out ok?" Janine asked the driver.

"We have a full tank and the package has been delivered," he replied.

"Good," she told him. "Let's get back to the church."

With a nod, the driver shut the door and drove the bus to the end of the block where he picked up the woman in green and then maneuvered through the city streets and back to the open road.

13. Delivered Unto Him

"We're going to die here aren't we?" Katie asked.

Mom didn't answer. Instead, she pulled a small pack from her pants pocket. Katie knew it well; it was Mom's rosary. She carried it everywhere she went. Katie carried one too, she had always admired her Aunt and wanted to be just like her. Katie pulled her own rosary from her backpack and together they began to pray. Dad and Uncle Brian continued scanning the room, searching for a way out. Aunt Eileen huddled in a corner, holding Lynn in her arms and sobbing. By the time they finished the first set of prayers, the batteries in Luke's lantern gave out. Unable to continue their game in the reduced light, Luke and Tommy put down their packs and joined Mom and Katie at the table.

Under different circumstances it might have been the signal of the end, but as a group they were resolute. At the conclusion of the second decade, Tommy's lantern faded and the darkness began to envelope them. With the only lantern that was still providing light Dad joined the group.

Uncle Brian approached Aunt Eileen, "Why don't you come over and join us?" he said as he took Lynn into his arms.

"What good is praying going to do? We're trapped and there's nothing we can do."

"We can have hope," Uncle Brian responded with a smile. He then helped Aunt Eileen to her feet and escorted her to the table adding their voices to the prayer.

The last light went out before the prayer ended, but this alone could not reduce the passion that everyone shared. Even the ending and the ensuing silence did not bring the fear back into the room. In fact, the mood became even lighter when Billy began to sing a tune he had heard at church many times before.

It had only one word, Amen. And that one word sung in a beautiful harmony reverberated in the chamber and helped to lighten the darkness. Billy didn't stop when the church version would have ended, he kept going and actually got louder. Then Luke joined him as did Dad and Mom and everyone else. The song became so consuming that they never heard the sound of the hatch opening, but Uncle Brian saw the light at the slide and in an instant he pounced on the person who slid into the room.

Luke thought it must have been No Neck, based on the size of the man that Uncle Brian forced into a stronghold, but the yelp that came out could only belong to one person. There, lying on the floor in Uncle Brian's powerful arms, was Uncle Al, gasping for breath, flailing his lantern and trying to keep Uncle Brian from finishing him off.

Everyone cheered when they realized who it was. They swarmed Uncle Al with hugs and Aunt Eileen broke out into outright sobs.

"How did you find us?" Mom asked.

But before Uncle Al could answer, Dad interrupted, "We can talk about that outside, let's get out of here."

"Wait!" Uncle Al said. "The tunnel collapsed when I was coming in; you can't get out that way."

"We'll dig," Uncle Brian said and he and Dad headed for the slide.

Uncle Al stopped them. "Wait, there's something I need to do before we leave."

No one wanted to stay one minute longer in this underground prison, but everyone immediately went silent when Uncle Al held up the blue glow of his cross. He then approached the stained glass window of Jesus Christ and inserted the cross into the window in the exact spot where Luke had pointed out the image. At first they thought that the floor was moving but it wasn't the floor, it was the stained glass window that opened to reveal yet another hidden passageway. This one led to steps, which Uncle Al climbed and everyone followed.

They emerged in the basement of the run down church. By the time they got outside it was very early in the morning and the first break of light had yet to change the sky. Everyone was overjoyed. They thanked God and breathed deeply the fresh air they thought they would never feel again.

Mom threw her arms around Uncle Al and squeezed him tight. "How did you know where to find us?"

Uncle Al stammered. "I didn't."

Everyone looked on in stunned silence as Uncle Al explained.

"I was doing research on Soren Jacobsen when I discovered the religious background of the Jacobsen family. When I found out that Soren had been working on a project for the church, I remembered the stained glass windows in this chamber. I returned to see if I could find any more clues."

"You mean you weren't following us or Janine?" Aunt Eileen gasped. "It was just dumb luck that you came when you did?"

"I wouldn't call it dumb luck," Katie defended. "I think it was all part of God's plan."

Everyone stood silently, contemplating the series of events and timing that made everything turn out the way it did. What if Uncle Al had gotten there two days earlier or if he arrived a week later or if he had never done the additional research at all. Several hands quickly made the sign of the cross, blessing themselves at the thought.

"So how do we get off this mountain?" Dad inquired.

Uncle Al pointed to the side of the church where an old World War II era motorcycle was leaning against the wall. "I came here on that; I can head down to the nearest village and come back with a ride."

No one wanted to see Uncle Al leave, but it was the only way. Before he departed, he pulled a water bottle and some food packs from a leather satchel on the bike and gave it to Dad. The food tasted like sweet nectar even though it was just beef jerky and crackers. The water was not enough for everyone, but fortunately Uncle Al knew of a stream not far from the church where they could get fresh water.

As the motorcycle zoomed down the road, they watched him race off and marveled at everything that had taken place over the past couple of days. It would be a while before he would return with a pick-up truck to take them back to Buenos Aires. The sun had already revealed itself and everyone was very tired, but a magnificent change had occurred in each and every one of them.

"Now I understand what Grandpa used to say," Luke said to no one in particular.

"What's that?" Mom asked.

"He used to say 'Every day is a gift from God.'" Luke paused to let the words sink in. "Before I used to think it was just a nice saying but now I understand what he meant." Luke really did know what it meant. Not only was every day a gift from God, but every hour, every minute and every second as well.

Even though Uncle Al was gone for over an hour, everyone was so consumed with the food, the water and the fresh air that they hardly had a chance to even check out the church and the surrounding area before he pulled up in an old beat up flatbed pick-up.

Uncle Al sat up front with Mom and Aunt Eileen while Dad and Uncle Brian sat in the back with the kids. Luke, Katie and Tommy tried to talk over the sound of the rattling shocks and revving engine. Lynn and Billy kept trying to stand up in the moving vehicle only to laugh hysterically when the bouncing of the road would cause them to fall over. Each time, either Dad or Uncle Brian would catch them, keeping them from any harm.

"Do you still have your passport?" Uncle Brian asked Dad as he caught Lynn in a bear hug.

Dad lifted his shirt and patted a small pack secured beneath his belt. "Yep," Dad responded, "I'm glad you suggested keeping them in these. I guess we'll never see our other bags again."

Uncle Brian laughed. "Eileen was so proud of her new Prada bag, she's never gonna let me forget about losing that." Uncle Brian turned to Luke, Tommy and Katie, "Do you guys still have your passports?"

Immediately all three rifled through their backpacks, one by one they each pulled the documents from their packs and showed them to Uncle Brian and Dad.

"So what are we going to do?" Luke asked Tommy and Katie. "We can't let Aunt Janine control the clock."

"She can't as long as your Uncle Al has the cross," Katie replied.

"But still," Luke answered, "that's all that's stopping her from controlling the clock."

"We don't even know what it does," Tommy interjected. "For all we know it doesn't do anything."

They all pondered the possibilities. Each one wondering what Aunt Janine had in her diabolical plans and what they could do about it.

Uncle Al drove them directly to the US embassy where they said their goodbyes. He promised to see them again real soon, but he still had things to do in Argentina and would not be able to make the trip with them. Everyone gave long and emotional goodbyes until Dad pulled them away.

It took quite a bit of finagling and Dad had to max out his credit cards, but with the help of the US consulate they managed to secure nine tickets to the United States. The trip home was not direct. They had to first travel to Miami, spend a night there and then catch a plane to Philadelphia. By the time they walked in the front door it was Sunday night, the same Sunday they would have returned had they really gone skiing in Quebec. And there, sitting on the dining room table, was another mysterious package.

14. Back to the Chamber

With a rumble and a screech, the white bus jolted to a halt in front of the old church. Janine was the first one off. Not waiting for the others, she headed down the hill and through the cemetery, arriving at the mysterious square of tombstones. The others, weighed down by supplies and equipment, struggled to keep up.

Again they went through the routine of pressing down on headstones until the tombstone moved and the passageway opened. No Neck crawled in. Abigail tried to follow, but quickly backed out. "The tunnel has collapsed," she announced.

"What do you mean?" Janine hollered.

No Neck emerged covered in dirt and confirmed Abigail's assessment. "It's closed off," he said, despair covering his face.

Janine didn't wait for No Neck to move; she made a hand signal to the women, "Go back to the bus and grab the shovels." Lunging into the hole she began clawing at the dirt. After ten minutes of intense digging, she backed out of the tunnel. "We need to come up with a plan. We can't let them die in there."

No Neck dove back into the hole and assumed Janine's position in the tunnel. With fury he burrowed in the dirt, pushing the loose gravel behind him. Abigail moved into the mouth of the opening and pushed the loose dirt out while The Walrus and Kerri moved it away from the entry.

Janine turned to Heather, "If we can measure the distance and direction, we can dig down into the tunnel further ahead." They motioned to the women in green who had just returned from the bus with shovels in hand. Janine paced the distance and directed the women where to dig.

The work was hard and took hours. No Neck made the most progress. He needed rest, but his thoughts of the trapped children would not allow him to stop.

The women in green had no success, the first pit they dug was stopped by impassable stone. The second must have been off course because they went down and down but did not reach any tunnel. They were about to start digging in a third location when they heard a cheer from Kerri and The Walrus. No Neck made it through. He didn't wait for everyone to catch up. Instead, he entered the first chamber and manipulated the dial in the center of the floor until the door opened.

While No Neck was turning the dial, Abigail entered and flooded the room with light. Abigail pushed on the opened door and slid her body inside. She marched down the corridor and repeated the motions on the dials on the doors at the end of the hallway, opening the trap door.

"It's all right," she called down the slide. "We've come to get you out." She waited a couple of moments for the others to catch up and then hurled herself down the slide with her lantern in hand. The light cast odd shadows throughout the room, but it didn't matter how much light she had, she was alone, at least until the others came tumbling in.

Janine was the last to arrive. She picked herself up and brushed the dirt from her clothes. "Where are they?"

No one had an answer. The chamber was filled with an awkward silence.

"They didn't just vanish into thin air!" Janine shouted. "They went somewhere; everyone start searching. Maybe there's a dial that opens another passageway."

Abigail and Kerri felt the walls, every crack over every square inch, searching for any signs. The Walrus and No Neck did the same on the floor, scanning every stone tile for something, anything that might lead the way out.

In her frustration, Janine grabbed a chair and hurled it at one of the stained glass windows, the picture of Jonah and the whale. She was amazed that despite the force, not even the tiniest crack emerged. She felt the surface. It was as smooth as ever. She continued to caress the smooth glass until her finger found a small sliver of an opening. She picked at it with her manicured fingernails; it was an odd shape, it had a curve, but it was not a circle. Janine dropped her bag to the floor. She pulled out a small knife and inserted it into the crack. She pried and pried at the opening until the tip of the knife broke off. Grunting with disgust, she moved to the next window, the image of Moses parting the sea. Again, she ran her fingers across the smooth glass. This time when she reached Moses' staff she found another crack, a shape that she recognized. She retrieved the rod from her bag and inserted it; a perfect fit.

Adrenaline coursed through her veins. She moved to the image of Noah and the ark. She found the opening in the window, removed the cog from her bag and placed it into the perfectly matched hole. By this time all the others had stopped what they were doing and were watching intently. Janine repeated the process at the other windows. She found a match for each image until she got to Jesus on the cross. With her hands on the window she found the cross shaped opening. Looking up to the ceiling in resigned disgust she shouted, "Albert!" Then turning to her crew she said, "It's time we find my dear husband."

"But where?" Heather asked. "We've been trying to find him for years."

A smirk came across Janine's face. "We'll get those kids and *he'll find us*."

15. Returning Home

Luke wondered what the next step would be. As much as the time in the chamber was terrifying, the thought of the bigger picture was consuming. How Luke, his mother and his brothers were a part of something much grander, something that was written about long ago, was surreal.

He thought the mysterious package was going to offer a clue. Filled with excitement he tore at the wrapping but was quickly disappointed when he found a pair of boots, with a note from Uncle Al wishing Dad a happy birthday. The challenge was set; he was going to have to start from scratch.

How difficult could it be to learn more about Soren Jacobsen and his inventions? Certainly the school library or even the University library would have lots of information on such a great inventor. Luke intended to find out.

It was difficult falling asleep for Luke. For everyone else, it was difficult getting up. Luke was driven, driven by the desire to know more about his future. He woke Mom and Dad, which was unusual. He tried to wake Tommy, but it was no use. Sleep had finally caught up with him and he was not going to let go so easily.

Luke dressed in a hurry, dragged a comb through his matted hair, ate a quick bowl of cereal for breakfast and headed off to school. He didn't remember the bus ride, his mind preoccupied with everything that had happened over the last couple of days. It remained that way until his third class and a chance to visit the library. His first stop was the reference computer to see what he could find. Surprising, for such an accomplished inventor, there were no listings for Soren Jacobsen. Not in the school library, nor in any of the libraries in the county system. A few quick keystrokes revealed that the school library had a few books on Denmark. He jotted down the reference numbers and headed off to search.

They weren't hard to find, but they did not offer what Luke was looking for, population estimates, average rain fall, languages spoken, currency used, and maps of the region. All useful information, but Luke needed more. He wanted to know about Soren, Hans and how his family fit into the picture.

For the next couple of weeks Luke tried Internet searches and visits to the local University, but still found nothing. He was beginning to wonder if Soren Jacobsen really existed or if Janine had changed the name to keep people from discovering her true intentions. Luke tried other searches on everything he knew about Soren, the clock, the magical pieces and the crossbow that he made for the king, but still he found nothing.

One day in the school library, searching additional phrases in the computer, he was about to give up when Miss Whiteman, the school librarian, approached him.

"Hi Luke, you look down, why so glum?" Luke was one of her favorite students. She loved any student who had a passion for books and Luke's near obsession put him at the top of her list.

"I'm trying to do some research, but I'm not having any luck." Luke frowned dramatically. Miss Whiteman was the best researcher he knew, but normally she would only point a student in the right direction; she would never answer questions directly. Luke was hoping for more today.

"What is it you're studying?" she asked.

"I want to know more about Danish history," he responded, "but our library doesn't have what I'm looking for."

"Have you tried the Atlas?" Miss Whiteman recommended.

"I looked at the maps," Luke replied. "I've checked all the books here and even at the University. I know the statistics, but I need to know more."

"Do you mean like the culture?" Miss Whiteman asked.

"Well," Luke paused, "is culture the same as legends and lore?"

"That sounds rather deep," Miss Whiteman laughed. "What class are you doing this for?"

"No class," Luke answered. "I just want to know more about my ancestry."

This peaked Miss Whiteman's curiosity. She loved helping kids find things for homework, but when it was for something beyond school she would really dig in. She always encouraged self-motivated research. "What is it you want to know?"

"There are legends and folklore that I want to know about," Luke explained. "The kind of stuff that doesn't show up in these," he said, holding up a few books from his backpack.

"Have you seen what other libraries in the network have?"

"Yeah," Luke responded. "They barely have anything. I had to go all the way to the University to get these, and even these don't have much."

Miss Whiteman gave it some thought and then said, "Have you thought about a personal interview?"

Luke was intrigued. "What do you mean?"

Miss Whiteman grinned. "I mean talking with someone who lived in Denmark?"

"That would be great," Luke said, "but I don't know anyone who lived in Denmark."

With a big smile on her face Miss Whiteman replied, "I might just know someone. My father is a butcher and he has told me about a woman who comes to his shop. Maybe I could put you in touch."

"That would be great!" Luke said with renewed enthusiasm.

The bell rang and Luke had to move on to his next class, but he had hope, now that he had Miss Whiteman's assistance. The hours plodded along with no word until he was heading for the bus at the end of the day.

"Luke," Miss Whiteman called out, "I have something for you."

Luke turned to her. Miss Whiteman's face beamed as she handed him a piece of paper. "Her name is Mrs. Johansen; here is her address. She can meet with you on Saturday if you have the time."

"I'll make time!" Luke said excitedly. He didn't know what was planned for the weekend, but he knew he was going to do anything that he could to meet with this woman, his best chance at learning about Soren Jacobsen and the mysteries of Danish lore.

On the bus, Tommy waited for Luke. "What was that all about?" he questioned.

"I think I have a lead," Luke smiled holding up the piece of paper. "Miss Whiteman gave me the name and address of a women who might know more about Hans and Soren Jacobsen."

"That's awesome," Tommy replied. "Maybe we can go see her tonight?"

Luke shook his head. "She can't see us until Saturday."

"But that's my karate tournament, I can't go then, it's regionals."

Luke's thoughts were far away as he absentmindedly answered, "Maybe Katie can go with me."

The two sat and stared out the window, Tommy thinking about his tournament and Luke thinking about the next step in their grand adventure.

16. A Little Help in the Investigation

Luke and Katie stood by their bikes in front of the little brick house. It had seen better days. Large overgrown bushes covered the lower half of the walls. A brick path struggled to be seen through spreading weeds. Old peeling paint hung off the pillars of the dirty front porch.

"Are you sure you want to go in there?" Katie asked.

"If we want to find out more about Soren Jacobsen I think we have to," Luke said.

The pair set their bikes down on the front lawn, moved up the sidewalk and stepped onto the porch. The screen door gave a loud squawking creak when Katie opened it. Luke rapped his knuckles against the old wooden door. It only took a moment and they heard noise from the other side. The door swung open to reveal an old thin woman, with grey hair and wrinkled skin. She was hunched over at the waist, with a curve in her spine that made it look like she had a hump on her back. A lit cigar dangled between her pursed lips. "Vat do you want?" came the rough voice in broken English.

"We came to see Anna Johansen," Katie answered.

"It's Mrs. Yohansen and who are you?" the old woman barked.

Luke spoke up, "Uh... Mrs. Johansen... my name is Luke and this is Katie. We're doing a project on Denmark and Miss Whiteman, our school librarian, said you could help."

With the mention of Denmark the old woman's gruff exterior changed to a modest gesture. "You vant to know about Denmark? Well, vy didn't you say so?" Opening the door she ushered them in.

The inside of the house was nothing like what they would have expected. It was pristinely kept with fine furniture and beautiful delicate objects. Based on the outside of the house, they had expected a dirty run down place, but this was like stepping into a museum of fine antiquities.

She hobbled along, struggling to move her old bones, leading Luke and Katie through her dining room. There was a large table that was set for a fine meal with place settings of china, silver and crystal at every seat and fresh cut flowers in the middle. Katie couldn't help but notice how beautifully the table was presented. They emerged to a back room with windows from floor to ceiling that overlooked a perfectly groomed back yard. Wicker chairs with cushioned seats were arranged to face the beautiful setting.

"Ah," the old woman said to them in her thick accent. With a sparkle in her eye she added, "You ask about the history of Denmark, but that is not vat you vant to know."

"It's not?" Katie looked at Luke and motioned that she thought the woman was out of her mind.

Mrs. Johansen gave her no notice. In fact she disregarded her altogether and focused all of her attention on Luke. "So vat is your name young man?"

"Luke," he responded, uncomfortable with this women focusing so much attention on him.

She shook her head vehemently. "No, no, no, your family name? What is it?"

"It's Stolin," he answered.

"No!" Mrs. Johansen denied him. She approached and inspected him closely. She gathered in his features and examined his hair. "Stolin is not a Danish name," she scolded him, "but you have Danish blood I can tell. Vat is your mother's name?"

Luke paused before he answered. "Bjorn."

Her eyes lit up. "Ah, Bjorn," she said in her native tongue. "Now I see it." She then turned to Katie. "And you," she said gruffly, "you have it too? The same Bjorn blood?"

Katie only nodded her assent.

Luke was fascinated by this woman, when she spoke it was captivating. When she said Mom's maiden name, it was unlike anything he had ever heard before. It sounded right. It was like she was speaking a foreign language and he understood every word.

Mrs. Johansen became much more engaged. She motioned for Luke to sit down and began to tell her story. "It's not the history of Denmark that you vant to know. You want to know about the legend."

"The legend?" Luke sat forward in his chair. Even Katie perked up as she heard the passion bubble out of the old woman's words.

"Yes, the legend. The legend of Holger Danske."

"Holger Danske?" Katie asked.

Mrs. Johansen brushed off Katie's interruption and continued to focus her story telling on Luke. "Before I begin, vould you like some candy?" She reached into her side table drawer and pulled out a small white box. "It is from the old country; the finest marzipan money can buy."

She opened the box and offered a piece to Luke. They were shaped like different fruits and looked rather tasty. Luke picked out one that looked like cherries and popped it in his mouth. Katie leaned forward for a piece, but Mrs. Johansen snapped the lid shut and put the box away before she could reach it. Luke, in the meantime, was greeted with what is known as an acquired taste, a taste that he had not yet acquired. The waxy candy was not sweet, in fact it was wretched, filled with a foul liquid that oozed a disgusting flavor to every taste bud in his mouth. He struggled to be polite, to not spit out the very gift she had so generously offered. With a big gulp, he swallowed it and offered her a gracious smile.

She loved it. She seemed to know that he did not like it and reveled in his strained efforts to remain polite. Her respect for him grew. With a pat on his knee she said, "You came here to ask about Holger Danske and I am going to tell you about Holger Danske.

"There are good men and there are great men, but there is only one Holger Danske. He is the greatest warrior the vorld has ever known. He has never lost in battle and to this day can never be defeated."

"To this day?" Katie questioned.

Mrs. Johansen did not acknowledge her, instead, with her attention focused squarely on Luke, she continued,

"Holger Danske is of royal blood, a leader among men and a true hero of Denmark. One day, Charlot, the son of the King of the Frankish Empire, attacked Holger Danske's only son and killed him. Holger Danske was enraged, but knew as a leader of the Danish people that there was a proper way to handle such matters. He sent a message to King Charlemagne explaining the events and asking for justice. King Charlemagne was outraged at the accusation, killed the messenger and sent his men to kill Holger Danske.

"Holger Danske had no choice but to defend his native land against the Franks. With his magical sword, Curtana, by his side, Holger Danske went off to fight the King's men and find King Charlemagne and his son. Holger Danske caught up with Charlot, but before he could capture Charlemagne he was called away. The Danish people needed him to make peace with Charlemagne and defend the land against the giant Brehus, and so, for the good of the Danish people, he took his magical sword, Curtana, and went to help the people of his homeland. Once again Holger Danske emerged victorious, saving the Danish people in their time of need."

Mrs. Johansen paused to see if she had Luke's full attention, but it was not necessary. He was at the edge of his seat, hanging on every word. Katie, too, was waiting in baited breath for the story to continue.

Mrs. Johansen went on, "Having fought off all of Denmark's enemies, Holger Danske returned home and fell asleep with his sword, Curtana, at his side. To this day he sleeps and dreams about all the events going on in our homeland and vaiting for the time when he will be needed again. And every Christmas Eve an angel of God visits him at midnight and tells him that all that he has dreamed is true and that he can continue his sleep; his services are not yet needed."

Luke was stunned by the story. He felt a connection with everything this woman said; he couldn't explain it, he just knew it deep down inside.

Katie was more skeptical than ever and having heard enough said, "That's great, but we really came here to talk about Soren Jacobsen."

"It's Yacobsen," Mrs. Johansen corrected her and gave her a cross look. She stood up and as she was leaving the room, she asked over her shoulder, "Who do you think made Curtana?"

Luke and Katie sat silently stunned as Mrs. Johansen walked to the dining room. Turning back she pointed at Luke. "You...You I like. You can come back. But your friend," she said with a thumb towards Katie, "leave her behind." And with that she left. It took them a while to figure out that Mrs. Johansen was not coming back. After several minutes of confused waiting they picked themselves up, walked out the door and rode their bikes home.

17. Running In To Old Friends

A small private jet skidded to a halt on the remote airfield runway. The stair door lowered and Aunt Janine exited with the other members of her crew in tow. A gangly man in overalls and a knit hat was there to greet them. "We don't get many planes like this here," he guffawed, taking a moment to spit the juice from his chewing tobacco to the ground.

Janine grimaced at the sight of him. "Is our limo waiting for us?"

"Nicest one I ever seen," the man replied.

"So where is it?" she demanded.

"Civilian vehicles aren't allowed on the runway," the man answered. "I'll take you back to the hangar," he said, pointing to an old Volkswagen minibus. "Doesn't look like much, but it gets the job done."

Janine signaled for her crew to get their bags and she headed toward the vehicle. He was right, it didn't look like much, rusted sides and broken side mirrors. The interior wasn't much better with ripped seats and stained carpet.

"Give me your coat," Janine said to The Walrus.

Reluctantly he removed his jacket and handed it to her. She laid it on the seat before sitting down. Despite the covering, she still cringed when the springs creaked beneath her weight.

The man opened the back hatch for their luggage. When he spotted Abigail he rushed over to help her, taking extra time to stare. When the last of the luggage was loaded into the van he slammed the hatch shut and rushed to the driver's seat. He barely waited for the door to close when he hit the gas and the minibus jumped forward. It jerked every time he shifted and bounced with every bump on the runway. It was obvious from Janine's expression that she couldn't wait for the ride to be over. When they pulled up to the hangar, a long black limousine awaited their arrival.

A man in a black suit approached. "My apologies Ms. Harmon, they wouldn't let me meet you at the plane." He escorted her to the limo and opened the door to let her in. "Bottled water in the refrigerator and caviar in the tray just as you instructed," he said. He then scooted to the back of the vehicle, opened the trunk for the crew to place their bags, and then returned to the driver's seat. Opening the window between the front and back, he asked, "Any change in the destination?"

Heather, who was seated closest to the front informed him, "Proceed as planned," and then with a flick of her finger closed the divider.

The limo drove through winding roads, with farmland as far as the eye could see. After a few minutes of driving, the scenery changed to spacious houses and then changed again to suburban sprawl with recently built housing developments and strip malls on either side. The country road quickly became a busy thoroughfare. Just a few minutes more and the houses got closer together and the town of Hartsville lay before them. The luxury vehicle turned off the main road, crossed an old steel bridge and turned into the driveway of the Stolin residence. The limo stopped and the driver popped out to open the door for Janine and her crew.

Janine marched up to the front door with her crew in lockstep behind her. She raised her hand to knock on the door when Luke and Katie rode up the driveway on their bikes. They skidded to a stop next to the limo. When they realized who was standing at the front door, they froze in their tracks. Janine laughed a hearty laugh, which made them even more nervous. She stepped down from the stoop and approached them. Luke backed up hesitantly, using his arm to protectively push Katie behind him. Janine's crew spread out to form a semi-circle around them. Luke looked in all directions, evaluating his opportunities for escape.

"Not to worry," Aunt Janine said. "I'm not here to hurt you, I came to make you an offer."

Katie shouted at Janine over Luke's shoulder, "Is that why you trapped us in an underground tomb?"

"You were never in any real harm," Janine responded with a smile. "We just wanted to keep you safe until we returned."

"Yeah right," Katie retorted.

"It's true," Janine said, taking a step closer and changing her tone to match that of a loving mother. "We're family. I would never want anything to happen to you guys."

Everyone's attention was diverted to a car pulling into the driveway. It was Uncle Brian and Tommy returning from their karate tournament. Tommy jumped from the passenger seat and joined Luke and Katie, prepared to fight. Uncle Brian was right behind him, and the crew responded by moving away from him and behind Janine.

Janine addressed her next line to Uncle Brian. "We don't want any trouble. We came here to make an offer. We'll tell you our plan and you can make your decision."

"What, no tranquilizers and handcuffs this time?" Uncle Brian said, taking an assertive step toward No Neck who backed away immediately. Uncle Brian's fists were clenched and he was ready to pounce. Katie stepped behind her Dad while Luke and Tommy moved to either side of their uncle.

Janine tried to calm the situation. "Why don't we go inside and talk to my brother-in-law and sister-in-law?"

Just then the front door opened and Mom came barreling out of the door. She raced down the steps and made a beeline for Aunt Janine. No Neck tried to step in front of her, but when he raised his arms to grab Mom, Uncle Brian threw a flying sidekick into his back, sending him sprawling onto the front lawn. With No Neck out of the way, Mom tackled Aunt Janine hard, landing on top of her on the driveway. Complete chaos ensued, Tommy lunged at Heather, sending her reeling, and in two quick moves Uncle Brian flattened The Walrus and Abigail.

Kerri backed away, pulling a tranquilizer gun from her pack and pointing it at Uncle Brian's chest. "Enough!" she shouted.

Heather, No Neck, The Walrus and Abigail were slow to get up. Janine was still pinned to the ground by Mom.

"Let her up," Kerri demanded, "or your brother is going down."

Reluctantly, Mom let Janine out of her grasp. The entire crew gathered around Janine and they moved toward the limo. As the others got into the limo, Janine addressed Mom and Uncle Brian, "We really did come here on peaceful terms. The clock and the pieces won't work without you."

Katie yelled, "Why should we help you?"

Janine turned to face her, and in a solemn tone said, "Because it's your destiny." She then placed a large envelope on the ground at her feet and backed away toward the limo adding, "All the details are in here. Take a look and you can give me your answer."

Mom stepped forward. "You've made your offer; now leave."

Janine stepped into the limo. "But will you come?"

"Just leave," Uncle Brian demanded.

"That's fine," Janine said, closing the limo door and peeking her head out the window. "We'll leave. But I'm going to call tomorrow for your answer."

In a matter of seconds, the car backed out of the driveway and headed over the bridge. Mom bent down, picked up the envelope, and ushered everyone back to the house, keeping her eye on the road and the limo that moved slowly down the road and out of sight.

18. Family Discussions

Everyone shuffled into the house. Uncle Brian closed the door firmly behind them and looked out one more time to make sure that Janine and her crew were truly gone. "That woman is crazy," he said to the others.

Mom paced the floor, adrenaline surging through her veins. Luke looked at her in awe and wonder. He couldn't believe she had manhandled Janine in such a way. But as he would find out, when it came to the defense of her children, there wasn't much Mom couldn't or wouldn't do.

Katie stamped her feet, crossed her arms and began pacing in Mom's footsteps. "Can you imagine? She thinks we're going to help her."

To everyone's surprise, Tommy stepped forward. "I'd like to see what's in the envelope."

Without a pause from her pacing, Mom handed the envelope to Tommy. He tore at the clasp and pulled out a stack of papers. "They're plane tickets," he explained, "and an itinerary for a trip."

"To where?" Luke asked.

Katie stopped her pacing and stared at Luke. "Like you need to ask? You know they're for Denmark."

Tommy nodded and held up the bundle for everyone to see.

Uncle Brian took the pack of tickets and turned to Katie. "How did you know where they were for?"

"Because that's the next stage of the journey," Katie answered. Turning to Luke, she asked, "Do you want to tell them?"

Before Luke could respond, Mom cut in, "Because Janine wants Curtana."

Luke and Katie stared at her, eyes wide in disbelief. "You know?" they asked.

"Yes," Mom admitted. "I know all about Holger Danske and his magical sword."

"But how?" Luke inquired.

"Same way as you I imagine," Mom replied. "When you find out you're part of an ancient legend, you become motivated to learn more."

"That's how you know how to read Danish!" Tommy said to her in amazement. "Did you know all this was going to happen?"

Mom shook her head. "I didn't know *this* was going to happen." She began to explain, "I only knew what Janine told me. That and what I read in FaFa's letters. Now I see it all coming to life before my eyes."

Uncle Brian stepped forward. "Wait! How about we take a step back and fill me in. I seem to be missing something here."

Katie started to explain. "A long time ago, when Aunt Lena and Janine first met, Janine made a lot of predictions. About how Aunt Lena would have three sons and their names would begin with the letters L, T and W. And how they would be a part of something that would change the world."

"I know about that," Uncle Brian said, his gaze not on Katie but instead peering steadily at his sister. "What did you mean when you said 'letters from FaFa?'"

Mom hesitated for a moment as if trying to decide her next course of action. Every eye in the room was fixed firmly on her. After a lengthy pause in awkward silence, she made up her mind. She crossed the floor to the fireplace and grabbed the clock on top of the mantel, turning it around and opening the back. From beneath the clocks' inner workings she withdrew an old fashioned key. With the key in hand she motioned for everyone to follow her into the dining room.

"When Uncle Brian and I were very young our grandfather died. He was our father's father; that's why he was called 'FaFa.' Well... when he died, he left each of us something special. Your Uncle Brian got his old desk and for me he left this dining room set," she said, pointing to the antique table and chairs that so beautifully furnished the room. "He also wrote each of us a letter. And in my letter was this key," she said, holding up the key she had just taken from the clock.

Uncle Brian sat down at the table. "I thought that key didn't open anything."

"For years I didn't think it did," Mom explained as she got on her knees by the serving sideboard. She opened a door and began pulling out her fine china, placing it on the table. "But one day I was cleaning and I found something." With the key in hand she reached into the cabinet, stuck it into a hole in the back and turned it gently. A panel in the back of the sideboard shifted and sprung open. She reached around and pulled out a bundle of old papers from the hidden compartment. They were tied with a string and yellowed from age.

"When Janine and I first met, we were very close. She used to spend countless hours telling me all sorts of stories. I wrote those in the book that I shared with Katie in Argentina. But I never told anyone about these." Untying the string, she separated the envelopes. "Well I didn't tell anyone but your father. I didn't put it all together, but he did. To me, Janine's stories just seemed like fun and fantasy, but your Dad thought for sure that she was talking about the same things that FaFa's letters were about."

Mom paged through the pile, stopping at one envelope near the top of the stack marked with a folded corner. Withdrawing the letter, she translated the writing from Danish so everyone could understand:

> "I visited her again today. I know everyone says she is crazy but to me she is fascinating. Today she told me that my blood will help free Curtana. Can you imagine? I know I shouldn't believe her, but when she talks, it's like I am taken to a faraway land."

Paging along in the letters, Mom stopped at another further down the stack, also marked with a folded corner. Again she translated her grandfather's writing.

> "She is beginning to show her age. Her sayings are more cryptic and harder to

understand. Today all I could make out was one name, 'Soren Jacobsen'. Research has been hard to find, but I am sure that this is the name she kept repeating. I'm going to get to the bottom of this. I have to; I feel connected to it."

Mom grabbed the next envelope in the pile and pulled out the letter.

"Today I went to the museum and they made a reference to 'Soren Jacobsen'. I couldn't believe my ears. I had to stop and ask the curator more. He said Soren was a great inventor, but when I tried to ask him more he said he was a great inventor, but other than that, very little is known about the man. I feel like I'm getting closer, but still very far away."

Again, Mom flipped through the pile, getting closer to the bottom of the stack. This letter she pulled carefully from the envelope. It was worn more than the others, like it had been handled much more often.

"Today she told me the strangest thing yet. She said my blood is tied to the legend of the Great Dane and that our paths will cross and history will be made. I am more confused than ever. I thought I was searching for Soren Jacobsen, but everyone knows about the legend of the Great Dane. At first I thought there must be a mistake until I learned about his sword."

Every eye was glued on Mom and every ear hung on every word. No one noticed the front door open behind them.

"So I guess we're going to Denmark," Dad said, startling everyone.

Uncle Brian turned and swung, but Dad ducked his punch. "Calm down Brian," he said from the floor. "It's just me coming home from work."

After they calmed down from the initial shock, everyone was relieved to see him.

"How long were you standing there?" Katie asked.

"I just walked in," Dad replied, straightening up and looking warily at Uncle Brian.

"Then how did you know about Denmark?"

Dad exhaled a deep sigh and looked across the room at Mom. "Your mother and I have been waiting for this day for a long time. When I saw her reading from FaFa's letters I knew."

All eyes turned to Mom. "I was getting to that." Reaching for the last envelope in the pile, she held it up and looked back at Dad. "Maybe you should read this one; you know how I get."

Dad walked across the room and took the envelope from Mom. He removed a crinkled page and began to read.

"If you have read these letters then you know the importance of all this and know what must be done. It won't be easy and will require great sacrifice, but it is our family obligation to see this through. The future of Denmark and the world as we know it depends on us."

"But Holger Danske can't be alive," Katie challenged. "That was hundreds of years ago and besides, it's just a legend."

"It may be a legend," Mom answered her, "but my grandfather, your great grandfather wrote these over seventy five years ago and everything is falling into place just as he said."

19. One More Time

The decision was made. Just like that, no discussion and no arguments. Everyone understood it was what needed to be done. Janine would not relent, and besides, each and every one of them felt intimately involved -- and indeed they were.

Uncle Brian went light on details when he was describing the trip to Aunt Eileen. She never would have agreed had she known everything. Katie knew this, which is why she kept completely silent while her dad explained about the wonderful opportunity to travel to Denmark for the Christmas break.

Back at their house, Luke and Tommy prepared checklists of things they would need, studied maps of where they were going and packed and re-packed bags for the trip. But most of all, they wondered what was in store for them in this far off land.

Mom was in a controlled frenzy. She bounced around the house with a clipboard in one hand and a whistle in the other. She barked orders like a drill sergeant, intent that they would be prepared for whatever might come their way. Dad was just the opposite. His mind was not on the trip at all. It was difficult for him to leave work, he felt obligated to get as much done as he could before they left. This meant he left for work every morning before anyone got up and came home after everyone was in bed. This went on for two solid weeks until the night before their trip.

Luke and Tommy sat in their room making last minute preparations. A stack of items was in the middle of the floor and they were debating whether or not to bring each. Luke held up a flash light, "You can never have too many flashlights."

"True," Tommy responded, "but we've already packed one for each of us and we need to make room for other stuff. Like the Swiss Army knives," he said, pointing to the two matching multi-function tools in the center of the floor.

"But what good will they do if they get confiscated before we get on the plane?" Luke said.

Tommy agreed and the Swiss Army knives were placed in the 'no go' pile. "Are we going to have any weapons at all?"

"Not unless we can buy them there," Luke replied.

Tommy thought about where they might be able to buy knives and nunchucks in Denmark, but it seemed like a long shot. Then he gave a sly smile. "What if we found a way to hide them in our luggage?"

"Yeah," Luke smirked, "and we can start the trip by being arrested for terrorism. That would be great!"

"Ok, ok," Tommy agreed.

"Are you bringing your iPod?" Luke asked.

"Are you kidding?" Tommy laughed. "It's a long long flight; you're going to need it."

"I guess you're right." Luke put his iPod in the 'pack' pile and then looked at the remaining items. There was a pair of walkie-talkies, a couple of notepads, a first aid kit and a mini tape recorder. Luke gathered up the whole pile and dropped them into his backpack. He turned to Tommy and said, "I want to take the journals."

"Yeah, and the Danish-English dictionary," Tommy added.

While Tommy picked up the dictionary from the night stand, Luke grabbed a flashlight and crawled under his bed. In the corner, at the point where the wall met the floor, Dad had installed a very special hiding place for the boys. When they first moved into this house a couple of years ago Luke and Tommy were very upset about leaving their old house and friends. So Dad built them a secret agent safe, to make the new house more fun.

In the corner beneath the bed Luke shone the flashlight at the baseboard. Rising up from the board, barely visible, were two small finishing nails. These nails acted as holding pins and when Luke removed them, a small piece of the baseboard fell away, revealing the front of a safe. With a few quick turns of the dial Luke opened the safe and pulled out several notebooks and journals, the things they had collected since this journey started back in September. Luke removed the journals, closed the safe, spun the dial, put the baseboard back into place and secured it with the nails. As he climbed out from beneath the bed, he was wishing he had hid one of Uncle Al's gifts in the safe, away from Aunt Janine.

Once the journals were out, they couldn't help but page through them one more time. This started a conversation about everything that had happened and what might happen next, a conversation that continued deep into the night.

Mom came in to put a stop to the talk. "We have a busy day ahead of us and we leave for the airport at 8:am. You boys need to shut off the light and get to sleep."

Luke and Tommy shut off the light and ended the conversation, but it would be hours before either one of them would fall asleep.

Morning arrived and chaos ensued. Everyone was late getting up and the limo driver was out front honking his horn. Mom was flying around the house like a mad woman, trying to get everyone ready. Dad was still trying to finish some last minute paperwork in his office and Mom was not pleased that he wasn't helping as she got Billy dressed, prepared breakfast and packed the bags.

After several warnings from Mom, Luke and Tommy finally rolled out of bed, threw their bags over their shoulders, walked downstairs and out the front door. They loaded their bags in the trunk of the limo and hopped in the back seat. Mom was annoyed that they hadn't brushed their teeth or combed their hair. All things considered, she was lucky they were dressed.

Mom ran out the front door with Billy in tow. Dad was right behind, weighted down with more bags than he could carry. The limo driver helped Dad with the bags while Mom put Billy in the back seat, all the while giving Luke and Tommy nasty glances. Fortunately for them, they had already fallen asleep and were oblivious to Mom's glare.

When they finally pulled up in front of Uncle Brian and Aunt Eileen's house they were all waiting on the front step with bags ready to go. Uncle Brian started to ask Mom why they were late, but upon seeing her mood, decided not to press the issue.

The limo driver loaded all of Uncle Brian, Aunt Eileen, Katie and Lynn's bags and they were off to the airport. Billy and Lynn, excited to be together, started bouncing around the limo. Several times they fell on top of Luke and Tommy. Under normal circumstances, Mom would have corrected them and tried to settle them down, but she was still angry at the boys and was glad that Billy and Lynn wouldn't let them sleep.

The limo arrived at the airport with just enough time to get through customs and arrive at the gate as they were making the last boarding call.

The flight was long and the quarters on the plane were tight, but for the first time in several months, Luke was relaxed. It was out of character for him to be easy going and social, but that's exactly how he was, moving up and down the aisles making idle chit chat with just about everyone -- family, flight attendants and strangers included.

Tommy couldn't be bothered. He had his head buried in the Danish-English dictionary and would swat Luke away every time he got near. Luke was particularly enjoying the role reversal and took every opportunity to playfully annoy his 'little' brother. After a while Tommy lost his patience and landed a strong jab to Luke's ribs, putting an end to the playtime.

Mom and Aunt Eileen talked softly. The nature of the trip was not discussed, but instead, they talked about schools and PTA meetings and favorite recipes. Billy and Lynn sat on their laps, their eyes glued to a DVD player showing an animated feature about two field mice heading into the big city. Dad and Uncle Brian were out cold, taking the opportunity of a long flight to catch up on sleep.

A couple of rows away, Luke caught Katie's eye and motioned for her to meet him at the back of the plane. She took out her ear buds, turned off her iPod and stood up. The man in the aisle seat gave her a disapproving look as she scooted by. Outside the window at 30,000 feet they could see the tops of clouds and a sun that was about to set. People around the cabin dropped shades and turned off lights.

In the rear of the plane near the restrooms, Katie met up with Luke. A nearby flight attendant shot them dirty looks for being out of their seats, but said nothing.

"What's up?" Katie asked.

"Nothing," Luke said. Pointing to her shirt he asked, "What's that?" When she looked down he raised his hand and bopped her on the nose.

Katie stepped back. "Cut it out!" she exclaimed.

Luke laughed at her and then asked, "Seriously, which of the people on board do you think are working for Aunt Janine?"

Katie, still bothered by the nose poke, was slow to answer. "What do you mean?"

"You know she bought us the tickets. I figure she has people watching us."

This made sense, but it made Katie very paranoid. She looked furtively about the cabin. Could it be him? Or her? This could be maddening.

Luke leaned in to Katie and slowly raised his hand. "What is that?" he said, moving his hand towards her chest. Again she looked down and again he bopped her playfully on the nose.

"I thought that you wanted to talk about something important, but all you want to do is annoy me." Not wanting to be the subject of his taunting, she turned on her heel and headed back to her seat. But now she was silently wondering who could be watching her. She got to her aisle and once again disturbed the man in the aisle seat. 'Could he be working for Janine?' she thought. It made sense; why not put someone in the seat right next to her? What better way to keep an eye on things? Katie was now consumed with suspicion.

In the back of the plane, Luke looked around the cabin for his next subject when he noticed an older woman staring at him. She looked away when he first made eye contact, but soon enough she was shifting her head to spy on him again. During a protracted moment of eye contact, she raised a pointy finger and motioned for him to join her in the empty seat beside her.

Luke looked around the cabin and, seeing everyone nodding off, decided, 'Why not?' He crossed the aisle, approached the woman and introduced himself, "Good evening Ma'am."

She may have been the oldest woman Luke had ever met. Her hair was silvery gray and her skin had more wrinkles than his fingers after swimming. Her eyes were soft and brown and looked like she could cry at any moment. She wore a cardigan sweater that was buttoned up to her chin and she smelled of moth balls and mints. In a scratchy voice that was barely audible she said, "She'll be waiting for you when you get off the plane."

20. Meanwhile

"Everything is going just as planned," Janine said as she closed the binding on the old leather bound book and lifted her head, a sinister grin enveloping her face. "How long before their flight touches down?"

From the other side of the room, eyes glued to her computer screen, Abigail answered, "It's on-time and scheduled to arrive in two hours."

Janine's crew was holed up in the suite of a luxury hotel. This was their headquarters while in Copenhagen and it served its purpose. Sitting at the conference table, Abigail and Kerri worked intensely on laptop computers. On the opposite side of the room, No Neck sat on the couch surfing channels on the television. The Walrus was next to him, complaining that he wouldn't stay on one program.

Heather was in the kitchenette preparing a pot of coffee while Janine paced back in forth in front of the big window, with views of the city behind her.

No Neck got up from the couch. "Do you want us to meet them as they get off of the plane?"

"I don't want to scare them," Janine said. "Send the limo to bring them to the hotel. We'll meet up with them later."

"What if they change plans and don't go to the hotel?" Heather asked.

"They'll go," Janine answered. "They've come this far; they're as curious as we are."

"What makes you think the clock will work this time?" Kerri asked. "Aren't we going to have the same problem we had in Argentina?"

"We know more now," Janine replied, patting the book they had acquired from the museum. "Plus, we won't be missing any pieces. Speaking of which," she turned to Kerri and asked, "What's *his* status?"

"He just crossed the border," Kerri answered without looking up from her computer.

Everything was indeed going according to plan. Janine was very pleased with herself. Years and years of dedication and hard work was finally coming to fruition. She could feel it, and the excitement made her tingle. In less than twenty four hours they would capture their prize. It almost seemed too good to be true.

21. Above the Atlantic

The words did not shock Luke. He was expecting Aunt Janine and her crew to be waiting for them when they got off the plane. It was Janine who provided the entire itinerary. But what was interesting was how this woman knew about it. Surely Aunt Janine would not place a feeble old woman as her lookout? Sitting down in the empty seat, he asked, "How do you know so much about it?"

"I've been around the block a time or two in my day," she replied with a gleam in her eye. "I can see things like this," she added, placing her right index finger knowingly on her temple. "Its part of the wisdom that comes with age."

Luke was baffled and not sure what to say. For more than a moment he sat there wondering. Does this woman work for Aunt Janine? Is this woman psychic? He contemplated what he should ask.

"Go ahead ask," the woman prodded him. "I know you want to know."

"What's going to happen to us?" Luke blurted. He wasn't afraid. In fact, he was excited. He had never at any time felt this way before. It was a feeling of doing exactly what he was meant to be doing. A feeling that everything in life made sense.

"Well I'm not sure of that," the woman answered. "She will be there for you because you are very important to her, that I can see. But as to what the future holds, that remains a mystery."

"But you can see why I want to know?" Luke asked.

"Sure," she replied. "No one wants to get hurt, but when it comes to these things, sometimes you have to take a leap of faith."

"A leap of faith?" Luke choked on the words, not sure he could put his complete trust in Aunt Janine. "That's an awfully big step."

"Love always is."

Luke looked at her strangely, "Who said anything about love?"

"You didn't have to," the woman said. "I can tell by the way you look at each other." Tapping Luke on the knee, she pointed across the cabin to where Katie was watching them from her seat.

"We're not in love," Luke injected. "She's my cousin."

"But I was right." The woman laughed. "You guys love each other and she'll be waiting for you when you get off the plane."

Luke got up and shuffled back to his seat, thoroughly disappointed with the way the conversation had turned.

Tommy was lying back and trying to get some sleep. "Where have you been?" he asked without opening his eyes.

"Don't worry about me," Luke responded. "We'll be there in a couple of hours; we should catch up on our sleep."

Tommy didn't need to be told twice; he was already snoring by the time Luke finished his sentence. Everyone on the plane was asleep. Everyone except for Katie who was wide eyed and shooting suspicious looks in every direction, searching for Janine's spies. Anxiously anticipating what would happen next.

22. Denmark

The flight landed in Copenhagen and after getting through customs they were greeted by a man in a black suit holding a sign that said "Stolin". Dad approached him and said, "We're the Stolin party."

"Very well," the man said in broken English. "I am to take you to your hotel."

"Sounds great," Dad told him and they followed him to the stretch limo waiting by the curb. Turning to Mom he added, "Janine may be a lot of things, but she certainly knows how to travel in style."

The kids were all excited to ride in the limo, playing with the power windows and the television set. They drank sodas from the minibar as they made their way along the cobblestone streets of Copenhagen. They gawked out the windows, admiring the beautiful parks and palatial estates of the "Queen of the Sea." All the while Dad regaled them with stories about the Vikings, Kierkegaard, and Hans Christian Andersen.

When they pulled up in front of the hotel they all jumped out and thanked the driver for the ride. Pulling their suitcases from the trunk, they headed into the lobby to check into the hotel. No one noticed the man in the corner hiding his face behind a newspaper.

Once they were checked in and had their room keys in hand, they headed for the elevator. Uncle Brian got on the first lift with Aunt Eileen, Katie and Lynn. "Give us a chance to get settled," Uncle Brian called over his shoulder. "We'll meet you at your room in thirty minutes."

The elevator door closed and the man from behind the newspaper approached. Before he could say a word Luke and Tommy bolted across the lobby, jumped into the air and wrapped their arms around him. "Uncle Al we're so glad to see you!"

23. Getting Answers

Someone knocked on the hotel room door. Before they could react, Uncle Brian pushed the door open and peeked his head in. He motioned to Mom and said, "Eileen and I are going to go for a stroll; we'll take Billy and Lynn with us. Make sure you catch me up on everything when we get back."

Mom was relieved. Since they finally caught up with Uncle Al there were a lot of questions they wanted answered and it was difficult when they were constantly tiptoeing around Aunt Eileen. Once Uncle Brian, Aunt Eileen, Lynn and Billy left, Mom gathered everyone together and they began to drill Uncle Al with questions.

"Where did you go when we left Argentina?"

"Why haven't we heard from you in a month?"

"How did you find us in Denmark?"

He tried to calm everyone down. Directing them to take a seat, he began weaving the tale as only Uncle Al could.

"When you guys left Argentina I still had some work to do." He looked about, to make sure he had everyone's attention. "From the airport I went to the museum in Buenos Aires. They had a collection of historical artifacts contributed to Soren Jacobsen. Unfortunately, by the time I got there the artifacts had been stolen. We can only imagine who was behind such a theft."

Everyone around the room mouthed "Janine," but no one made a sound.

Uncle Al continued, "When I was speaking with the curator about the missing artifacts he mentioned another museum in Paris that had contacted him about verifying the authenticity of some newly discovered relics possibly related to Holger Danske. He offered to let me tag along, so I was off to France.

"When we got to the museum in Paris we found a collection of letters detailing a most incredible story. It was a story that had been handed down through generations of a single family. As the story went, there were six Danish warriors who were childhood friends of Holger Danske. When the seven of them were old enough to defend the homeland, they all joined the military service and were placed in the same regiment. Holger Danske had saved each and every one of their lives in battle over their many years together. After his legendary battle with the giant Brehus and his return to Denmark, he fell into a deep sleep with the promise that if Denmark ever needed him, he would rise again. Every year an angel of God visits him and lets him know whether he is needed."

"On Christmas Eve," Luke inserted.

"That's right," Uncle Al said. "So you're familiar with the story?"

"A little bit," Luke replied, "but I'm still learning."

"That's great," Uncle Al said with a wink. "Keep learning, always keep learning."

"Well, his six childhood friends and fellow warriors made a pledge to defend the sleeping Holger Danske until he awoke. After several years of round the clock protection they realized that they could not protect him forever and devised a plan for his defense. They hired Soren Jacobsen to create the ultimate defense system.

"Soren built the clock which is the key to Holger Danske's protection. The clock will only work properly when brought together with the five magical pieces. As part of the plan, the six Danish warriors separated, each warrior traveled to a different part of the globe and, with the help of Soren Jacobsen, created his own hiding place. The warriors made a pact never to reveal the location where each piece was hidden.

"The warriors plan was to have Soren finish the project and then for each to depart to hide his piece. Soren, of course, could not be allowed to survive since he knew not only the secret of the protection, but also each of the hiding places.

"According to these letters, the sleeping Holger Danske was buried in a vault that can only be opened with the clock; the one we found in Argentina. Soren was also left inside the vault. He was left to die along with his assistant, a small boy of only five years old, Soren's great grandson, Hans."

Luke, Tommy and Katie looked at one another with mouths wide open. They returned their glance to Uncle Al and he was smiling and nodding along with them.

"But as we can guess, Hans did not die inside that tomb. He survived long enough to share with us the secrets that were meant to protect Holger Danske.

"This all took place at *this* fortress," Uncle Al said handing out a couple copies of a tourist brochure. "The castle of Kronborg. It's only twenty five kilometers from here.

"That's how I found you. I knew that Janine would be looking to get you guys to Holger Danske's tomb on Christmas Eve."

"As you can see in the brochure, they claim that this is where Holger Danske went into his legendary sleep. They have a monument to commemorate it." He pulled out a map from his satchel, opened it up and placed it on the table. "And here," he said, pointing to a spot on the map, "just off the coast by the fortress, is where a collection of Soren Jacobsen's artifacts were found by a group of divers. Not conclusive proof, but certainly more evidence that the vault that Soren Jacobsen created to protect Holger Danske is at this fortress."

Everyone sat in silence, contemplating everything that Uncle Al had just told them. This was truly incredible. The pieces of the puzzle were coming together and everything was starting to make sense.

"But what does Janine want? Does she really think Holger Danske will rise from the dead?" Dad asked.

"I don't think it's Holger Danske she wants," Uncle Al answered. "It's his sword."

"Curtana!" Tommy blurted out.

"That's right," Uncle Al confirmed. With a look of admiration at Luke and Tommy he added, "You guys really have done your homework."

The phone rang and Mom quickly picked it up. "Hello."

On the other end Janine said, "I'm glad you made it. How was the trip?"

"Fine," Mom answered stoicly. Their lives were intertwined now; Mom accepted that, but she didn't need to enjoy Janine's company.

Janine didn't mind, she preferred to keep all relationships about business. "You're here, so I'm hoping we can work together on this."

"We're here," Mom agreed and she left it at that.

"Good," Janine responded. "And I take it my dear Albert is there with you?"

Mom turned to look at Uncle Al. He correctly assumed that they were talking about him and gave Mom a nod of approval. "Yes he's here," Mom replied.

"Excellent," Janine said. "We need to go to Kronborg Castle tomorrow night. We'll pick you up in front of your hotel at 9 o'clock."

Mom replied, "Maybe it would be best if we meet you there."

Janine did not like this. "I think it would be best if we pick you up."

Ignoring Janine's last comment Mom said, "Fine, we'll meet you there then. Let's say outside the castle at 10?"

Janine was frustrated and tried to repeat herself, but Mom cut her off, "Oh that's great! We'll see you then, bye," and she hung up the phone.

If Janine were a cartoon character she would have had steam coming out of her ears and an exploding head. Instead, she seethed anger from every pore and sat in utter silence. No one in the hotel suite dared to say a word. They could tell by her end of the conversation that the call did not go as planned and Janine did not like when she was not in control. She sat for a protracted pause and then turned to Abigail. "I want them tailed. I want to know what they're doing and where they're going, understand?"

Uncle Brian, Aunt Eileen, Billy and Lynn came in from their walk and Uncle Al ducked into the other room, out of sight. Everyone stood around waiting for Mom to finish her call so they could find out what was happening.

Mom hung up the receiver and said to everyone, "We're going to get a night time tour of Kronborg Castle tomorrow night. We need to be there at 10 o'clock."

Uncle Brian understood exactly what Mom was telling the group. Aunt Eileen did not. But Uncle Brian still wanted to know more. "Hon," he said turning to Aunt Eileen, "why don't you take the girls back to the room, I'll be there in a minute."

"Sure," Aunt Eileen said, "so I can give baths and put them to bed by myself, I don't think so. You're coming now."

Uncle Brian rolled his eyes. Reluctantly he agreed with his wife and the four of them left the room. Mom immediately began to relay the details of the call to everyone. It was no surprise. They knew they would be going to Kronborg and that it had to be on Christmas Eve at midnight. By the time they finished discussing everything they thought might happen, there was a soft tap on the door. It was Uncle Brian. Dad and Uncle Al agreed to put the boys to bed so Mom could give him the update.

The night time ritual turned into a wrestling match. Uncle Al and the boys jumped on top of Dad and the jostling and wrangling continued until Mom walked in.

"I thought you were putting the boys to bed."

131

All of them froze. Uncle Al looked up from beneath Dad's headlock and jokingly said, "They are in bed."

Mom laughed, but everyone knew that play time was over. Uncle Al went back out to the other room where he made himself a comfortable spot to lay on the floor. Luke and Tommy layed down on one bed while Mom placed Billy in a rollaway cot next to the bed she and Dad would sleep in. Billy went from jumping on the bed to deep sleep faster than Mom could turn out the light. It didn't take any of them long to fall asleep, they had a very eventful day, but it was nothing compared to what awaited them.

24. Gathering Supplies

Mom got up early and ordered a gigantic breakfast from room service. She purchased just about everything on the menu. Why not, it was all being billed to Aunt Janine. Luke and Tommy woke up to the wonderful smell of bacon and coffee. Uncle Al, Mom and Dad sat at the table with full plates and contented smiles. Luke grabbed a plate and dug in, as did Tommy. They ate scrambled eggs and pancakes and French toast and hash browns and fruit Danish, stuffing their bellies until they couldn't eat any more.

A loud cry startled everyone. Mom was the first one up and she rushed to the other room to find Billy, crying and shaking in the darkened room. He woke up and didn't know where he was. One look at Mom and he was relieved, back to his normal devilish self before Mom could even get him dressed.

At the breakfast buffet Uncle Al was having fun, distracting the boys with a slight of hand trick while simultaneously stealing their bacon. They laughed and screamed and it turned into a wrestling match with Luke and Tommy tackling their uncle onto the couch.

Dad had his head buried in a travel guide, busy planning their day. "So what would everyone like to do today? It's Christmas Eve, we're in Denmark and we don't have to be anywhere until ten tonight. What do you say we go sightseeing?"

Luke and Tommy stopped their assault on Uncle Al but stayed on top of him as they listened to Dad. Tommy knew what he wanted to do. He wanted to find a martial arts store so he could be prepared for tonight, but he didn't want to mention it to Mom or Dad. He decided it would be best to wait until he was alone with Uncle Al and ask him privately.

Luke rolled off of Uncle Al, grabbed a map from the table and opened it up. "What do you think about going to the castle today?" he asked.

Mom came in from the other room. "But we're going there tonight," she said as she fixed a plate of eggs, toast and fruit for Billy and led him over to the table. He took some food but refused to sit, instead, preferring to eat while he wandered around the room.

Luke was focused. "Wouldn't it be a good idea to check out the place before tonight so we know what to expect?"

Mom and Dad looked at one another and grimaced. How could they argue? They had things they wanted to do today, but he had a point. All at once their whole day was changed from being a fun tourist to a busy worker, they were more than a little disappointed.

A knock on the door startled them. Dad looked through the peephole to see Uncle Brian, Aunt Eileen, Katie and Lynn. He opened the door to welcome them in.

Uncle Brian stepped forward. "Do you guys want to go out for breakfast?" he asked.

"We ordered in," Mom replied, stepping forward with a cup of coffee and a plate.

"Great," he said, grabbing the plate and heading for the table. "I'm starved."

Aunt Eileen took the cup of coffee. "Isn't that kind of expensive?"

Mom didn't want to mention Aunt Janine in front of Aunt Eileen, so she just shrugged and said, "It's our vacation; you only live once."

Everyone around the room froze. Mom never said or did things like that. Although it was strangely out of character for Mom, Aunt Eileen didn't seem to notice. Katie took a muffin and went over to where Luke and Tommy were having a quiet conversation with Uncle Al.

"So do you know where we could find one?" Tommy asked in a hushed tone.

"I think I may know a place," Uncle Al answered.

"What are you talking about?" Katie asked rather loudly.

Luke shushed her and motioned for her to sit down. He then whispered in her ear that Tommy wanted to find a weapon to take with him tonight and Uncle Al thinks he knows where to go.

"I bet my dad would want to come too," Katie replied with no caution to her volume. It was true, as Luke and Tommy's Sensei, Uncle Brian had taught them all about how to fight with weapons, but as their uncle he had taught them a love of all things that go crash and boom. He liked that stuff as much or more than they did.

"We're going to have to find a way to go without anyone getting suspicious," Uncle Al said.

"No problem," Katie replied. She crossed the room to her parents and said, "Mom, Dad, Uncle Al knows about a local dojo, can I go with them?" Katie knew this would have two effects. First, Aunt Eileen rolled her eyes and said, "Can't we have one vacation without karate?" And then Uncle Brian said, "That's great; when do you want to go?" And just like that they were headed for the door.

For the first time Aunt Eileen noticed Uncle Al. "Hey, what are you doing here?" she asked.

Uncle Al and the kids turned to her but weren't sure what to say. Mom cut in, "You didn't know he lives in Denmark now?"

Aunt Eileen looked at him with a strange expression on her face, thinking back to the last time she saw him. Before she could say anything Mom offered, "You know Eileen, they have a wonderful spa at this hotel. I was thinking that John and I could watch Billy and Lynn if you wanted to go get a massage."

Everyone waited on Aunt Eileen's response when Mom added, "you could charge it to our room, we wouldn't mind." Mom turned to Dad who nodded in agreement.

A smile came across Aunt Eileen's face, "Well if you wouldn't mind..." Before anyone could say another word she was out the door and headed toward the elevator and the spa.

The group released a collective sigh when the door shut behind her. "We're going to have to tell her sometime," Mom said to Uncle Brian.

"We will," Uncle Brian responded. "How about tomorrow?"

"But we're going to Kronborg tonight?" Tommy said.

"Exactly!" Uncle Brian responded.

Outside of the hotel, Uncle Al sidled up next to Katie. In a soft tone he told her, "We're not going to a dojo."

"I know," Katie replied, "I just said that to make sure my Mom didn't come along. If she thought we were going shopping, she'd be leading the way."

Uncle Al looked at Katie with a new appreciation.

"Where we're going is only a couple of blocks away; we can walk," Uncle Al told the group. They strolled down the sidewalk checking things out as they passed.

"Dad," Katie called to Uncle Brian, "we're not really going to a dojo."

"We're not," Uncle Brian said in feigned surprise.

"No," Katie answered, "we're going to a place that sells karate equipment."

Uncle Al interrupted her, "That's not really true either."

"It's not?" Uncle Brian and Katie both said.

"Not really," Uncle Al explained. "The place where we're going sells a lot of different things."

"What kinds of things?" Uncle Brian asked suspiciously.

Uncle Al looked at Uncle Brian and then Katie, Luke and Tommy. They all waited for his response. "Back home you might call it a pawn shop." He paused for a moment before continuing, "But here, they refer to it as a black market boutique."

"Oh," Uncle Brian said. This was not the answer he was expecting, but it didn't stop him from moving along the path towards their destination.

There was not much activity on the sidewalks or in the stores. Just about everything was closed for the

Christmas holiday with the exception of a few cafes. They passed a restaurant with empty tables on the sidewalk and reggae music coming from inside. Just past this cafe they turned down a narrow alleyway. Uncle Al led the way with Luke, Tommy and Katie right behind him. Uncle Brian brought up the rear, constantly looking over his shoulder. The tight confines made him nervous.

About halfway down the alley, Uncle Al stopped. There was a steel door that had no markings or windows. On the frame next to the door there was a buzzer that Uncle Al pressed once and then waited. After a couple of minutes he rang the buzzer again, only this time he held it for more than a couple of seconds. Behind the door they heard footsteps and a grouchy voice barking, "Roligt jeg kommer." A small slide opened on the door and a pair of eyes peeked out. "Hvad onsker du?"

"Kenneth, det er me, Uncle Al."

A grunt from the other side of the door let him know that he was not expected, but the slide went shut and the steel door opened. There stood a man you could tell had seen hard times. His brown eyes were opened wide like a man who was constantly in a state of fright. Luke and the others would learn that this was a permanent look. He had fought in many wars and had survived near death experiences in every one of them. He had seen friends die and he had killed enemies. And all of these things could be seen in his hardened face. He wore army boots, faded jeans and a black t-shirt with white lettering that said "Mistes!" 'Get Lost' in Danish. The hair on the top of his head was very thin and his face had the scraggle of a man who hadn't shaved in days, but could never develop a full beard or moustache. His lips curled when he spoke; every word dripped with disdain for life and everyone in it. Uncle Al started to move forward, but the man stopped him before he could enter. In heavily accented English he said, "Who are they?"

Uncle Al laughed. "These are my nephews Luke and Tommy and their cousin Katie."

"Who is he?" Kenneth asked about Uncle Brian.

"He's her father," Uncle Al said. Then to reassure him added, "Don't worry, he's with me."

"What makes you think I don't worry about you?" Kenneth replied, but he stepped aside and allowed them to enter.

When Uncle Brian caught up with Uncle Al he said, "What kind of place did you bring us to?"

"You'll see," Uncle Al answered.

They walked through the first room. It was piled high with old televisions, computers and stereo equipment. There was no order or arrangement. It was just storage. The next room had a little more organization to it. In this room there were metal shelves along each wall and on each shelf were boxes labeled in some unknown language. They did not stop in this room either but passed through to what looked like a regular shop. Glass display cases filled with a variety of items formed a u-shape. Kenneth stepped behind one of the cases, sat down on a stool and barked, "So vat are you looking for?"

Uncle Al stammered for a second and then said, "We're looking for something from your private stock."

Kenneth glared at Uncle Al. "I don't know vat you are talking about."

Tommy made a quick glance to Uncle Al. "Did we come to the wrong place?"

Uncle Al raised a hand, motioning for Tommy to be patient. Before he could speak a loud buzzing sound filled the air. Kenneth looked at Uncle Al. "Are you expecting someone?"

"No, are you?"

"I vasn't expecting you," Kenneth grumbled. "Nowadays I never know who's gonna be at my door." Getting up from his stool, Kenneth scolded the kids, "Don't touch anything." Then he crossed the floor and headed to the door.

Luke, Tommy and Katie took the opportunity to check out the items in the display cases. This guy had everything you could possibly want. There were war medals, police badges, necklaces, bracelets, watches and rings. There were cameras and camcorders and tools for almost anything you could imagine and some you could not. A pendant caught Katie's eye. It was round and made of gold and had twelve stones set around the perimeter, each stone representing a month of the year. Luke checked out some interesting tools while Tommy searched, but was disappointed to find that among all these items there was not one weapon.

Uncle Brian motioned for Uncle Al to meet him in the corner. "This isn't a pawn shop; this guy deals in stolen merchandise."

"Have you ever been to a pawn shop?" Uncle Al responded.

Uncle Brian didn't respond, but it was obvious that he was uneasy.

Kenneth returned from the front door and handed Uncle Al a piece of paper. It was a photo printed from his security camera. "Do you know these guys?"

25. A Trial Run

Uncle Al took a long look at the photo before answering, "No," then handed the picture to Uncle Brian. "Do they look familiar to you?" The picture showed two men dressed in navy blue three-piece suits, each with their hair slicked back, close to their scalp. One of the men used his hand to block his face from the camera. On the back of his hand was an image of two winged dragons on either side of a fleur-de-lis.

"No," Uncle Brian replied, "should they?"

Kenneth was annoyed. "They came to my door just minutes after you got here. I don't think it's a coincidence."

"Is it one of Janine's goons?" Uncle Brian asked Uncle Al.

Uncle Al cringed when Uncle Brian said Janine's name in front of Kenneth.

Noticing Uncle Al's discomfort, Kenneth cut in, "Don't worry, I already knew Janine was here. I saw her a couple of days ago."

Uncle Al nodded his consent, but could not bring himself to look at Kenneth. "Did you guys make up?"

Kenneth glared at Uncle Al. "Enough to pay the bills," he retorted.

"What did she buy?"

"Let's just say I wouldn't want to be running into her," Kenneth answered.

There was silence in the room as each person contemplated what Janine could have bought here that would make her so dangerous.

"Now you see why we need your help?" Uncle Al said.

"Ok, ok," Kenneth replied. "Take them back to the other room."

Without a word, Uncle Al directed Uncle Brian, Luke, Tommy and Katie back into the room with the shelves. Kenneth closed the door for less than a minute and then opened it back up again. When they came back, one of the display cases on the left side wall had shifted to reveal a hidden doorway. They followed Kenneth into a secret room with his private stock.

This room was a warrior's dream. The left wall was covered with guns – handguns, shotguns, rifles and assault weapons. Every gun was displayed on its own rack and a locked cage on the floor held ammunition. There were two empty spaces among the assault weapons. Uncle Al pointed to the gap and asked, "Is this what Janine picked up?"

"Among other things," Kenneth grumbled.

Along the back wall there were collections of riot gear and a table of uniforms. The riot gear included several bullet proof vests, helmets, shields, gas masks and in the center of the wall a rocket launcher. The uniforms on the table were a variety of police uniforms and standard issue military garb in green, tan and camouflage. There were two empty spaces by the gas masks. When Uncle Al pointed to the space, Kenneth nodded glumly. Uncle Al's eyes shot to a shelf where the nerve gas sat. He didn't need to ask, the empty space on the shelf told him all he needed to know.

On the wall to the right there were two sets of shelves with hand-to-hand combat weapons. This is the section Tommy went to as soon as they entered the room. The collection included swords, knives, batons, throwing stars, nunchucks and more. Tommy picked up a pair of nunchucks.

"Careful with those," Kenneth warned him, "they aren't toys."

Tommy whipped the chucks around his body with great precision, a routine he had practiced a thousand times.

"You're pretty good," Kenneth admired. "Ever thought about going into the military?"

Tommy didn't provide a verbal response, but instead turned to Uncle Brian and bowed. This caused Kenneth to look at Uncle Brian with even more suspicion and contempt.

Kenneth turned back to Uncle Al and asked, "So vat's it going to be?"

"I think Tommy would like the nunchucks," Uncle Al said with a big grin. "How about you Brian?"

Uncle Brian didn't respond immediately, but his eyes were focused on a collection of throwing knives on one of the shelves. "I guess it would probably be good to have a couple of these."

143

Kenneth shook his head. "You already know Janine and her group left here with heavy hardware and you're looking at nunchucks and throwing knives."

"We're not killers," Uncle Brian answered.

"It's your call," Kenneth said.

"How much?" Uncle Brian asked, holding up the knives.

"Are you paying in dollars or kroner?"

Uncle Al cut in, "Let's put it on my account."

A grunt that sounded almost like a laugh escaped from Kenneth's lips. "Not if you're going after Janine; she doesn't like you so much anymore."

"C'mon," Uncle Al reasoned, "you know I'm good for it."

"You're only good for it if you survive. I want cash now."

There was a lengthy stretch of silence until Uncle Al finally relented. "Fine, but I want your best price." Turning to Luke and Katie he asked, "How about you guys, see anything you want?"

Katie smiled and said, "Nothing for me thanks."

"How about that necklace you were looking at earlier?" Uncle Al asked her.

"Really?" Katie was stunned, but in a matter of two seconds she bounced to the next room and returned with the round pendant with the twelve birth stones.

"Luke," Uncle Al asked, "how about you?"

Luke took a moment to think, "I don't think I need a weapon but I could use some of the tools I saw in the other room." Luke went back and returned with a laser measuring tape and a surveyor's scope.

By the time Kenneth and Uncle Al had haggled over the price of every item Tommy had added a couple of throwing stars to the list. Soon everyone had their stuff and they were on their way. The walk back to the hotel was filled with exciting chatter.

They made it back to the hotel lobby just in time to meet Aunt Eileen coming out of the spa. "There you are," she said with a relaxed smile. "How was everything at the dojo?"

Uncle Brian could tell that she was a little out of it. He wondered if they had given her some kind of relaxant. "Are you ok?" he asked as they walked toward the elevators.

"Oh yeah," she responded. "I just had the most incredible massage, manicure and pedicure." She held up her hands for everyone to admire her fingernails, but only Katie appreciated what she was showing them.

"Did you have anything to drink?" Uncle Brian asked.

"Just a couple of bubbly orange juices," she replied. Sensing his disapproval she said in a whisper that everyone could hear, "Don't worry about the cost, Lena said I could bill it to their room."

Uncle Brian knew that Aunt Janine was paying for everything, but he didn't let Aunt Eileen know. "That's great," he said. "Will you be ready to go to Kronborg this afternoon?"

"It seems silly to me," Aunt Eileen said. "If we're going for a special tour tonight then why do we want to go over there this afternoon?"

Uncle Brian didn't want to explain it to her. "You know you could just go this afternoon, that way you wouldn't have to go tonight."

"That's a good idea," Aunt Eileen responded, "but I think I'll pass on going this afternoon and just go tonight. The massage made me sleepy, I think I'll take a nap."

This is not what Uncle Brian wanted. He was trying to keep Aunt Eileen away from Janine and her crew, but that was easier said than done. At least they would be able to investigate this afternoon without arousing suspicion.

The elevator door opened and they moved down the hall. Dad was sitting on the floor in front of their suite, with his back against the wall.

"Is everything ok?" Uncle Al asked.

"Yeah," Dad replied. He stood up. "I just went to get a drink and I thought I would take a break before I went back in."

Everyone was confused until they opened the door and saw Mom chasing Billy and Lynn around the room. Everywhere they went, they left a trail of destruction, like a tornado through a trailer park. Mom was frazzled. When she heard the door she turned looking for help. "Where have you been?"

"Oh," Dad stuttered, then held out two cans of soda.

"How long were you gone?" Uncle Al asked him.

Under his breath Dad answered, "I left about five minutes after you."

Katie, Luke and Tommy sat on the floor and started a game which immediately calmed Billy and Lynn.

Aunt Eileen offered Mom an amorous hug, "Thank you for the spa day, that was great." Oblivious to Mom's disheveled appearance and ragged disposition she added, "I think I'm going to go back to my room and take a nap, that massage made me sleepy."

Mom was about to say something when Uncle Brian cut in. "Hon, why don't you take Lynn with you. It's about time for her nap."

"Okay," Aunt Eileen answered groggily. "C'mon honey, Mommy's going to take you back to the room for a nap."

Lynn protested, her whines could be heard all the way down the hall as Aunt Eileen took her back to their room.

Uncle Al got on the phone and made arrangements for transportation to Kronborg. Mom called room service and ordered lunch from the hotel kitchen.

Three taxis arrived to take them on their trip. Dad, Mom and Billy rode in the first cab, Uncle Al rode with Luke and Katie in the second and Uncle Brian and Tommy took the third. When they arrived at the castle they spilled out of the cars and gathered on the sidewalk. Uncle Al paid all three drivers and gave them instructions to meet them in three hours at the same location.

Everyone was awestruck at the enormity of the fortress. Walking through the front gate, they could feel the history. "How much of this castle stood here when Holger Danske returned from battle?" Luke asked. Everyone was too consumed with taking it all in to answer or even hear the question.

Mom spotted a line of tourists leading to a ticket window and she got in line. Luke noticed a group of art students with sketchpads sitting on the ground near the wall and went over to join them. In a matter of moments he had his own sketchpad out, only he wasn't drawing the architecture, instead, he was creating a schematic of the castle using his laser measuring tape for exact dimensions. Once he had the measurements of every wall, window and doorway he found a stairwell leading to the top of the fortress wall and climbed up. From here he could see for miles in every direction, overlooking the Oresound and Sweden in the distance. He used the surveyor's scope to check out the surrounding areas, making notes in his sketchpad.

Mom finally made it to the ticket window. The previous group had taken forever as they struggled to communicate with the woman behind the counter. Mom did not have any problems, She spoke fluent Danish and ordered tickets for everyone. She even haggled for a free ticket for bringing such a large group.

They signed up for a guided tour featuring the whole castle as well as a visit to the renowned statue of Holger Danske himself. A stern looking woman in a starched blue uniform addressed the crowd, "The tour is about to begin, if all ticket holders would please follow me."

When the guide began her speech, Mom was right in front glued to every word. Luke was half listening, but he was more interested in checking out all of the areas that were 'off limits' to all but castle employees. On several occasions, he was redirected back to the group by a security guard.

Uncle Al, who had been on this tour several times already, was not so interested. Instead he played games with Tommy, Katie and Billy. He had a small rubber ball that he bounced off of the stone block walls every time the tour guide wasn't looking causing Billy to laugh out loud. On more than one occasion the children were scolded for making too much noise and each time Mom gave Uncle Al a penetrating glare and then instructed Dad and Uncle Brian to get the children under control.

The castle tour led them up winding stairways and down damp corridors all the while the tour guide continued her oratory, highlighting famous paintings and sculptures, showing where kings and dignitaries had slept and explaining the story of how this fortress was a cornerstone of Danish history. She then led them out of the main building and back to the courtyard where they crossed the grounds to the Southern wall where they passed through a large doorway into a small lobby. They were getting close and everyone knew it. Luke's attention to the tour guide became very focused and Tommy and Katie stopped playing games. The moment they had been waiting for had finally arrived.

They walked from the lobby into a dimly lit hallway. At the beginning of the corridor they were able to walk side by side, but as they continued into the depths of the castle, the passageway got smaller and smaller until they were forced to walk in a single line. The pathway made several jutting turns and then it opened up to a larger cavern. Then they saw him. There, along the opposite wall sat a life size sculpture of Holger Danske asleep on his throne, helmet on his head, long flowing beard down his front and Curtana tucked neatly at his side.

Tommy made a couple of quick moves through the crowd to get a closer look. He was staring wide-eyed when Luke and Katie walked up next to him.

"This isn't it," Luke exclaimed.

"What are you talking about?" Tommy asked. "He's right there. All this time and we're finally in front of Holger Danske."

"I'm telling you," Luke insisted, "it doesn't feel right."

"What do you mean?" Katie asked.

"I'm not sure," Luke tried to explain. "Everything else we've been through, I could just tell. But I don't have that feeling in my gut."

Katie looked at Tommy for feedback, but he only offered a dramatic rolling of the eyes. Luke noticed it and reiterated, "I'm telling you this isn't it!"

The tour guide explained the story of the Great Dane, his battles, his return to Kronborg, his deep sleep and his promise to return if Denmark ever needed him. Her words reverberated off of the cavern's stone walls creating an eerie echo. Even though they had heard the story before they were captivated by every word. When the guide finished her explanation she gave everyone time to take a closer look. After about ten minutes she announced, "This concludes our tour of Kronborg Castle; we will now make our way back outside where you are welcome to stroll the courtyard or browse our gift shop."

One by one the group filed out of the cavern. Luke stayed behind, taking one more look at the statue.

"Still think it's not the right statue?" Katie asked.

"I'm telling you," Luke answered, "it just doesn't feel right."

"C'mon," Tommy called after them, "we need to catch up with the group."

Luke, Tommy and Katie bolted up the hallway to catch up with the others. They were pretty far behind and couldn't see anyone or even hear the tour guide. They turned a darkened corner when two sets of arms came out of nowhere and grabbed them from behind.

26. Making Preparations

There in the shadows of a side corridor were Mom and Uncle Al. "Shh, don't scream," Mom instructed them. "Dad and Uncle Brian took Billy out. They're going to distract the guide to give us more time."

"More time for what?" Katie asked still shaking from the shock of being grabbed in the dark.

"To do a little investigating of our own," Mom answered. She then pulled three flashlights from her bag and offered them to Luke, Tommy and Katie. They each shook their heads and pulled out their own flashlights. Mom looked at Uncle Al and they both smiled, amazed at their resourcefulness.

They made their way back to the cavern and the statue of Holger Danske. Uncle Al, Tommy and Katie used

151

their lights to check every section of the area, looking for anything unusual. Mom and Luke checked out the statue.

"Shouldn't there be a table?" Luke asked.

"What do you mean?" Mom responded.

"I don't know," Luke explained, "but I thought there would be a table in front of him."

"You're right," Uncle Al said. Moving across the room to meet Mom and Luke at the statue he added, "the legend says that his beard flows into the table before him. I wonder why I never noticed that before."

They stared at the statue in contemplative silence until a voice startled them from behind. "The tour is over and this exhibit is closed."

Mom responded with a well rehearsed dialogue, "Oh thank goodness you found us," she implored. "We got separated from the group and we didn't know which way to go."

Her words were well played, but the security guard wasn't buying it. He looked at each of them suspiciously before directing them to the corridor and then back to the courtyard.

Dad and Uncle Brian were waiting with Billy when they came out. They started to approach but backed off when they saw Mom shaking her head. The guard escorted Mom, Uncle Al, Luke, Tommy and Katie through the courtyard and out the front gate and in a gruff voice said, "And don't come back here again!"

Back at the hotel Luke, Mom and Uncle Al sat down to make plans for the night's adventure. They were determined to have the upper hand when they met up with Aunt Janine.

"There are two entrances into the fortress," Luke said pointing to the schematic laid out across the table. "And, there are five doors that lead from the courtyard into various parts of the castle.

Uncle Al interjected, "The land that surrounds the fortress is mostly water, so that limits the ways to approach, ... or escape."

"While we were on the tour I picked up another map of the castle," Mom offered, "it shows all of the inner workings of the fortress." She placed it on the table. "Together the maps and drawings give a pretty accurate description of Kronborg and its surroundings."

"Except for one point," Luke said, matching up his drawings with Mom's map. "Look, we pretty much know the whole layout of the castle except for what's behind this one door." He pointed to a door on his drawings along the south wall of the courtyard.

"That door doesn't appear on any of the maps provided by Kronborg," Uncle Al offered.

Tommy stood nearby whirling his new nunchuck around his body. They were lightning fast, just a blur in every direction.

"Tommy, can you move to the other room with those?" Mom asked. "Someone could get hurt."

Tommy stopped practicing and moved to the next room. He was thrilled that Mom didn't take away the weapons or even ask where he got them.

On the other side of the room, Dad sat with Billy, playing with a pack of Danish flashcards. Billy was picking up the language rather quickly.

A light tap on the door and Uncle Brian and Katie entered. "Eileen and Lynn are still asleep. We decided to let them sleep; it will be safer for them here," Uncle Brian announced. Everyone let out a deep sigh of relief. Hiding all of their plans from Aunt Eileen was exhausting.

Uncle Brian went into the other room to work with Tommy. He laid out his new knives on the bed to examine them more closely. Mom came in, but again she said nothing about the weapons. This time Tommy could have sworn he saw a smile on her face when she saw Uncle Brian with the throwing knives.

Katie joined Luke and Uncle Al at the table.

"It took a while, but I think we finally have a plan that will work," Luke said. "We get to Kronborg ahead of Janine and secure the superior positioning. If we can control the castle walls we should be able to get the upper hand."

A sharp rap on the door brought the conversation to a halt. Mom looked at her watch. "8 o'clock; we still have time." She looked at Uncle Al and mouthed, 'Janine?'

He shrugged his shoulders. "I don't know."

Uncle Brian walked silently across to the peephole and looked out. "Oh no!" he exclaimed.

"Is it Aunt Janine?" Luke asked. "Did she come early?"

Uncle Brian looked down and shook his head. He opened the door, Aunt Eileen and Lynn came bounding in. "Oh thank goodness," Aunt Eileen shouted. "We thought you guys left without us. We didn't want to miss all the excitement."

Aunt Janine and her crew didn't need to find them. Just one floor up in the same hotel they sat and watched every move, broadcast from tiny hidden cameras located throughout the suite. Aunt Janine already knew about their plans to get to the castle early and to try to get the upper hand. She also knew about Uncle Brian's throwing knives and Tommy's nunchucks. All of these things would make no difference. She summoned two women in green and gave them explicit instructions, "Here's what I want you to do…"

      Luke felt good about all of his research and the plan they came up with. The pride continued right up until Uncle Al, Katie and Mom fell over in mid-sentence. "Are you guys all right?" He rushed to Mom's side and lifted her head; she was lifeless. He turned for help only to see Dad, Aunt Eileen, Billy and Lynn slumped over. Uncle Brian and Tommy staggered in from the other room and fell to the floor. Luke didn't know what to do. He took one step towards Uncle Brian and his vision started to blur, his head felt light and the room began to spin. His knees buckled, he flopped face down on the floor. He kept his eyes open long enough to see two women, dressed in green and wearing gas masks come in through the door, followed by Aunt Janine.

      "Make sure you get the weapons," he heard Aunt Janine say. "Take these notes and bring their backpacks; we may need them."

      Luke's eyes failed him; all went black. His struggle ended with a single thought, "Not again."

27. Kronborg Castle

Smelling salts brought Luke, Katie, Tommy and the rest of the group back to the real world and their current predicament. They were all very groggy as Janine and her crew led them off of the bus and into Kronborg Castle.

Uncle Al separated from the group and approached Aunt Janine. "Hi cuddle bear, it's been a long time."

"Don't call me that," Janine retorted. "You know I hate when you call me that."

"Have you missed me?" Uncle Al asked with a sly smile and a sultry glance.

Luke and the others stared in anticipation. Abigail, Kerri and Heather also looked on, unsure of what to expect.

"As if," Janine replied, "I couldn't stand you then and I detest you even more now."

"Aw c'mon, how about a little kiss?"

"Well…" Janine offered a bashful smile and moved closer to Uncle Al and his now puckered lips. She leaned her face close to his and whispered, "This is for telling your family I was dead." And with blinding speed she grabbed him by the shoulders and rammed her knee into his groin sending him doubled over in pain.

Several "Oh's" and "agh's" emitted from the group. Dad moved to Uncle Al's side to help his brother.

Janine addressed her crew, "Enough wasted time, let's get moving."

One of the women in green used the barrel of her rifle to nudge Luke forward. Mom gasped when she saw her son treated this way, but Kerri's firm grip on her arm kept her from action. Luke didn't seem to mind. Instead, his eyes wandered about, his attention captivated by the architecture of this centuries old fortress. Every tower, archway and window carried its own magnificent story and he savored every detail, letting it all sink in. Just a couple of months ago he had never been out of his small town of Hartsville, Pennsylvania and now he had been to Quebec (although conscious for only a small part of his time there), Argentina (where he was trapped in an underground tomb) and now Denmark. This new stage of his life certainly wasn't safe, but it sure was interesting.

The courtyard, the center of the fortress, had four sides of high and solid wall. Each wall ran about three hundred feet long and a hundred feet high. There was a doorway in the center of each with a balcony above. The most prominent of the doorways was to the north and it had an elaborate covered balcony that overlooked the courtyard. There was no one up there right now, but Luke could envision this place hundreds of years ago with a lively market and privileged royalty peering down from their lofty perches.

The door to the north was large and ornate; it led into the castle. The doors to the east and west were large, but not as decorative. They were not headed for any of these doors, instead, they were directed to the door to the south, the door that led them to the statue of Holger Danske. As they got closer to the entrance, the woman in green redirected Luke to a small wooden door to the right of the southern doorway. Luke knew this door; it was the passageway from his schematic that was not on the Kronborg maps. It was in need of repair with peeling paint and rusted hinges. As they reached the door, the woman in green stepped in front of Luke, smashed the lock with the butt of her rifle, kicked the door open and shoved Luke into the small dark corridor. The walls were stone and damp from the sea air, the floor, uneven, with a steep downward slope. Luke had to lean back to keep from falling forward. He placed his hand out, steadying himself with a wall covered in mold and mildew.

A lantern was passed from the back of the line. Luke squinted his eyes and watched as the flicker of light cast wicked dancing shadows throughout the corridor. Without a word, he took the lantern and led the way down the dark tunnel. It wasn't too bad at first; the tunnel was tall enough that he could walk, and wide enough that he didn't feel confined. But after several twists and turns, the walls got closer, the ceiling lower and the stench of the salty sea air stronger. All the while the slope continued down, deeper and deeper beneath the fortress. The tunnel wound like a maze and got smaller and smaller until it became so tight that Luke had to crawl to get through. After twenty feet of crawling, he pushed the lantern through a small door that opened up to a vast chamber on the other side. Luke tried to check things out, but the minimal light from his lantern revealed little. He stood up and turned back to the opening where the remainder of the group filed in. One by one they emerged. Each person stood up and stretched, relieved to be out of the constrictive confines of the tunnel.

By the time the last person emerged, the collection of lanterns and flashlights filled the room with an ominous glow. It was an underground cavern with walls cut from the earth's natural stone. At the far end stood a statue, a large edifice of a sitting man with a long flowing beard spread over a table before him. He wore a helmet on his head and a large sword at his side. His eyes were shut, but he was a menacing figure nonetheless. This statue was very similar to the one they had seen on the tour, but somehow it was more real and more menacing.

Everyone stared at the statue in silence. Tommy broke the void with two words, "Holger Danske." He was right, but still, no one else said a word. It would be several moments before anyone would make a sound.

"Assume your positions," Janine barked. Her crew followed her orders, fanning out, creating a semi circle around the statue and forcing Luke and the others closer. The crew pressed inward causing everyone to come face to face with the chiseled likeness of Holger Danske himself. Janine did not move nor did she take her eyes off of the Danish warrior.

"What are we doing?" Tommy whispered.

Mom replied, "I think they're expecting something to happen at midnight."

With a wave of her hand, Janine set her crew into motion. Abigail placed her backpack on the table, unzipped the compartment and withdrew Soren Jacobsen's clock. Just like in the tomb in Argentina, the table in front of Holger Danske had a groove in the center that the clock slid into. No Neck steered Luke and Tommy toward the table while Kerri did the same with Mom and Billy. Heather motioned for Uncle Al to join them. All the while, the women in green kept their guns pointing menacingly at Dad, Uncle Brian and Katie. In the far corner, outside the circle, Aunt Eileen huddled with Lynn.

Janine pulled a notebook from her bag and opened it on the table. After a few moments of reading to herself she reached into the interior of the clock and touched the ring. It began to glow and emit a soft hum.

She motioned to Mom and pointed to a place inside the clock just below the ring, "Insert the cog here." Mom did as she was directed. Tommy then moved into place with the red glowing rod in his hand. He inserted the rod into the hole in the center of Mom's cog; both pieces glowed and floated together. Then Billy, with Mom's assistance, inserted the yellow glowing coin on the other end of the rod. An eerie silence filled the cavern; no one moved or even blinked.

"It's your turn," Janine said to Luke.

He knew. He had done this before and even then it had come to him instinctually. Luke picked up the fishhook causing it to glow green. He inserted it into the clock, attached one end to Mom's cog and the other to Billy's coin.

Now four pieces hovered in the magnetic field, five colors glowed brightly. All eyes turned to Uncle Al. The look on his face held confusion, fear and curiosity. He wasn't sure what would happen when he set the clock into motion and he worried about what Aunt Janine would do with them once she had what she wanted.

"It's time for you," Heather instructed Uncle Al.

He pulled on the string around his neck and lifted the cross from beneath his shirt. A blue glow emanated from his hand. Slowly he moved forward, lifting the cross to put it in place, but no further action was necessary. A powerful force pulled the cross out of his hand and joined it with the other pieces in the center of the clock. Together the pieces formed a single unit. A strange rotation set the gears of the clock into motion. The hands spun rapidly and then, for a brief moment, stopped. Then they spun again. This continued as the time reflected on the clock rolled on. Everyone watched with breathless anticipation as the time on the clock grew closer and closer to the current date. And then a loud CRACK! startled everyone in the room. The clock stopped and the walls and floor began to shake. The statue of Holger Danske began to move.

Mom pulled Billy close to her and backed away. Dad moved forward, wrapped his left arm around Luke and his right arm around Tommy pulling both of them away from the moving statue. Uncle Brian grabbed Katie and withdrew to the corner of the cavern where Aunt Eileen and Lynn were huddled.

Janine's crew stood motionless and dumfounded. But not Janine, with wide eyes and eager anticipation she approached the stone carving. Not only had Holger Danske moved, but so did the table and the chair he was sitting on. A large gap was revealed, a passageway into the unknown. Janine stuck her flashlight into the opening then turned to the women in green. She had a maniacal look on her face as she said, "We found it, it's really true."

28. Deeper

The two women in green moved to the opening.

"No! Janine stopped them. "Let them lead the way."

One of the women tossed a lantern to Uncle Brian and another to Dad and said, "You heard her, get going."

Aunt Eileen held Katie and Lynn as Uncle Brian moved toward the new tunnel. Dad met him there and said, "So is this what you thought we'd be doing on our vacation?" They exchanged nervous smiles then ducked their heads to enter.

"Wait!" Janine called out. She pointed to Luke and Tommy and said, "They should go first."

Dad protested. "They're just kids."

"They're the only ones who are truly safe here," Janine replied. She then motioned to the women in green to execute her orders. They did as they were told, taking the lantern from Uncle Brian and giving it to Luke.

Luke didn't hesitate and Tommy was right by his side. Together they entered through the gap. The tunnel sloped down at a very steep angle. Luke tried to go slowly, but the steep decline combined with the slick mossy substance on the floor and walls made it nearly impossible. He was slipping into who knew what.

"Luke, reach up," Tommy yelled, reaching out a hand. Luke grabbed Tommy's wrist while Tommy used his other hand to hold on to a ridge in the ceiling of the tunnel. For a minute he held him there. "Luke, I won't be able to hold you, your hand it's too slippery."

"Just let me go," Luke instructed. "I'll be ok."

"I'm not letting you go!" Tommy screamed. "You don't know what's down there."

"Trust me," Luke insisted.

"No," Tommy demanded, his voice reaching another level. "Just listen to me! Raise your right foot to the wall over there." Luke followed his brother's instructions. Tommy continued, "Now wedge your left foot over against the other wall." Luke did this and the weight was lifted.

Luke was able to support himself, but only for a little while. "My feet are slipping," he said.

"It's ok," Tommy said calmly. "Look at me."

Luke looked up.

Calmly Tommy instructed him, "Put your hand on the ceiling; there's a groove up there." Luke followed these directives and sure enough there was a ridge. In fact, beneath hundreds of years of mold, there were multiple grips fashioned in the stone. Holding onto these rungs,

Luke was able to lower himself down the sloping tunnel at a controlled pace. Tommy followed.

Luke and Tommy descended about fifty feet when Luke called back, "Tommy, the ladder has run out, but the tunnel hasn't. I think I have to drop."

"Don't do it," Tommy implored him. "Think of the last time; if you had dropped then you would have been killed."

Tommy's words made sense, but Luke just knew what he had to do. He tried to control his pace by wedging his feet against the walls like he did before, but the slime on the walls at this depth was much slicker and impossible to hold. He fell faster than he wanted to, but his landing was softened by several inches of grimy water at the bottom. The persistent sound of dripping water echoed throughout the cavern. Luke shone the lantern around. Even in the minimal light this was the most beautiful room he had ever seen.

This room was smaller than the cavern above, but its design was much more elegant, even palatial. There were six sturdy columns around the perimeter. Next to each column was a meticulously sculpted statue, each one depicting a different Danish warrior. Each warrior held an oil lamp in his left hand and a sword pointing to the ceiling in his right. The swords all pointed to the beautifully designed dome. On the ceiling, crafted from thousands of tiny color tiles, was the scene of Holger Danske defeating the giant Brehus. The detail was incredible. Luke could sense Holger Danske's inimitable power as he wielded Curtana, the giant in anguish at his feet.

At the far end of the vault Luke's light landed on a stone carving coming up out of the water. It appeared to be a foot. He raised the beam a little higher and saw that this was only a small portion of another statue of Holger Danske, this one much larger than the original. This statue was identical to the one up top with two exceptions. Here he did not sit on a chair, but instead, on a throne fit for a king and up top he sat before an empty table, but here his beard flowed into a table set with eight place settings of the finest gold goblets, plates and cutlery laid out in preparation for a feast.

"This is the place!" Luke called out.

Hearing Luke's words, Tommy let go, sliding down the tunnel into a splash. "Ugh, you could have told me I was going to land in water."

"Oh yeah," Luke laughed, but he never took his eyes off of the mammoth figure.

Tommy looked around and he too was speechless as he tried to take in every detail from the warrior statues to the ornate ceiling to the statue of Holger Danske himself.

There was commotion up above and soon two people came flying down into the vault. Based on the velocity by which they arrived, it was obvious that they did not slow themselves by grabbing the ladder or pressing their feet against the sides. It was a miracle that neither Kerri nor Abigail was hurt. Aunt Eileen and Mom were not so lucky. Aunt Eileen got her foot caught about halfway down and Mom came crashing into her causing the two of them to twist and contort in a tangled mess.

Kerri and Abigail were up in a flash, circling Luke and Tommy in an aggressive fashion. Tommy assumed a fighting stance, keeping the women at a distance. Luke was too occupied with the statue to take notice.

Up top, the women in green, under Janine's direction, forced the others down the tunnel. They did not take the time to tell anyone about the ladder or the dangers that lie below. Uncle Brian and Dad came barreling down, landing in a heap in the water. The kids were much more resilient. Katie, Billy and Lynn raced down the tunnel like a playground slide, spinning and splashing wildly. They got to the bottom laughing and giggling, ready for more.

Aunt Eileen's ankle was badly injured and Mom's shoulder was dislocated, but this did not keep them from stumbling forward to check on their children, pulling them close and hugging them tightly.

Janine, Heather and the two women in green were the last to arrive. No Neck and The Walrus lowered them slowly with a rope. The women in green immediately lifted their rifles and corralled everyone next to the statue. Janine stood up, brushed the debris from her backside and looked around. Abigail and Kerri circled the room, lighting the oil lamps held by the stone warriors. Once these lamps were lit, everyone could finally appreciate the immense beauty of this room, a masterpiece in its own right.

Janine's eyes lit up as she took in the incredible beauty. "All these years I've worked and finally I'm here." She then called back up the chute, "Send Albert down!"

No Neck and The Walrus looked around the cavern but Uncle Al was gone. They looked at one another, neither one wanted to be the one to report back. No Neck bolted to the tunnel that led back to the courtyard; Uncle Al was nowhere to be seen. "Should I chase after him?" he asked.

They were befuddled, unsure of what to do next. Both stood silent and motionless. Finally Janine called again, "I said send Albert down!" She paused and then added. "Can you hear me?"

Realizing that The Walrus was not going to respond No Neck moved to the passageway and called down, "We can hear you, but Uncle Al is gone!" He cringed, anticipating a harsh response.

Janine turned to Luke, "It looks like your dear Uncle Albert has abandoned you." She smirked and added, "I guess he showed that backbone of his after all."

Luke didn't know what to think. Would Uncle Al really take off without them? He couldn't hide the pained look on his face.

Triumphantly Janine turned away from Luke, her eyes coming to rest on the mammoth monolith. She was in awe. For decades she had studied and prepared for this moment, the discovery of Holger Danske's tomb. She never believed the tales, that he was not dead, but merely asleep. What she did believe was that this great warrior was buried with his sword, the greatest weapon of all time, and that this statue was the marker for his burial place. She examined every square inch of the room and the statue. She took extra time checking out the sword on the statue, what little she could see of it since it was tucked neatly into its sheath.

Janine was visibly disappointed. She turned to Heather, Kerri and Abigail and said, "There are no markings of a burial plot. They would not have buried him without marking the site according to the tradition."

"So what does that mean?" Abigail asked.

"This is not a tomb. There's no grave here and if there's no grave then there is no sword."

"What about the legend?" Abigail responded.

"Do you really believe that?" Janine mocked.

Abigail laughed. "I probably wouldn't have believed all this," she said, raising her hand to the tunnel and then the statue, "but here we are."

"Very well," Janine replied. Turning to the women in green she said, "You know what needs to be done."

The women in green both pulled 9mm pistols from their belts and pointed them firmly at the group. Dad and Uncle Brian stepped in front, shielding everyone else. Realization struck; they were going to die here. Janine no longer had use for them.

167

"Bang!" With one squeeze of the trigger and one deafening blast, a bullet hit Dad in the stomach. He doubled over in pain. The children screamed and cries filled the air.

29. Not Again

"Why did you do that?" Abigail started to run towards Dad but Janine stopped her.

"They were in danger and he didn't save them," Janine said as a matter of fact. "We had to test your theory."

"You didn't have to kill him." Abigail cried, tears streaming down her face.

Meanwhile Mom, Uncle Brian, Aunt Eileen and the kids huddled around Dad crying and screaming. He lay in three inches of water clutching his gut, blood gushing over his trembling hands.

While the children cried and Mom and Uncle Brian tried to treat the wound, no one noticed Janine and her crew gathering all of the gold from the table and retreating; using the rope to scale their way back up the tunnel. The only thing that gave them away was when the passageway up top closed with a bang.

Horror is the only word that can describe being trapped in an underground vault with no way to escape. They had been trapped before but this time Dad, Mom and Aunt Eileen were hurt and Janine made it quite certain that they were expendable; she would not be coming back. Their only hope was Uncle Al. Could he get help and find a way back into the tomb without the clock.

A painful silence filled the room, silent except for one sound, the incessant drip, drip, drip of leaking water. But as relentless as the drip was it could not drown out the grief and despair that sieged everyone's mind.

Mom huddled over Dad. Luke, Tommy and Billy looked on in disbelief. Uncle Brian managed to scale the wall and climb back up the chute, but he was back down in a few minutes confirming that the top hatch was sealed tight. He moved around the perimeter of the room, searching in vain for a way out. "The water is coming in, so it must have a way to get out," he rationalized.

"Uncle Al is out there," Luke stated confidently, "he's knows we're in here. He'll find a way to get us out."

Aunt Eileen sat on Holger Danske's foot, resting her injured ankle and holding Katie and Lynn close. "Is it just me," she asked, "or is the water getting deeper?"

She was right. In the time that they had been down here the water level had gone from just a couple of inches to reaching just below her knee. It was rising and rising fast. Uncle Al might be working to get them out but would he get back soon enough? As if the prospect of being trapped in an underground vault wasn't bad enough, now they were faced with the terror of drowning.

Uncle Brian came up with an idea. "If we can get everyone up the tunnel we can get away from the water."

"I can't climb with my ankle like this," Aunt Eileen said.

"I'm not leaving John," Mom replied, never taking her eyes off of Dad.

"Neither are we," Luke and Tommy added. Billy walked over and rested his head on Dad's shoulder.

Uncle Brian knew and understood, but his mind wouldn't give up. He continued his search, trying to find any possible way out.

The water continued to rise. Luke and Tommy helped Uncle Brian lift Dad, first onto the table and then up onto Holger Danske's shoulders. Everyone climbed into position. This was the highest point in the room. It kept them safe for a little while but the waters kept coming. Soon the level reached the stone warriors and their oil lamps. The flames were doused leaving only the dim light from Luke's lantern to fill the room. But still the water rose. There wasn't anything they could do. Mom tried to calm the others but it was no use.

When the water reached their bodies Billy and Lynn began to cry. "I'm cold," Lynn wailed. Billy cried. Luke tried to remain calm, hoping beyond hope that Uncle Al would find a way to rescue them before it was too late.

The water level moved up their bodies, first to their waists and then their chests until it was a struggle to keep their heads above the cresting tide; taking in water with every breath. Gagging and choking; spitting and gasping, trying for one last gulp of air. Another minute and it would be over. Time was running out.

Luke tried to get one last look at his family; his loved ones. Mom burst into tears when he looked into her eyes and mouthed the words, "I love you." Dad struggled to maintain consciousness, but was alert enough to give Luke a wink. Billy bawled in fright. Katie looked up from her father's shoulder just long enough for Luke to see she was crying uncontrollably. The water was above Luke's chin now and he needed to spit to clear his mouth just so he could take a new breath. He turned to Tommy, but Tommy wasn't looking at him, his eyes were focused somewhere in the distance.

Taking a large gulp of air, Luke submitted to the water. In the last second before the water rose above his mouth Luke heard something, it was Tommy yelling.

"Holger Danske!"

In that same instant a whirl of blinding light rose from beneath them. Is this what death feels like? The blinding light turned into a whipping force that circled above their heads and then drove down through the water creating an earth shattering smash. Everything gave way; all senses were lost.

30. After the Fall

The fall was intense. For a couple of seconds Luke was floating in mid air and wondering what happens after death. But then the feeling changed to a rush of extreme speed as his body hurled downward at a breakneck pace. The free fall ended with an abrupt crash and an enveloping feeling of extreme cold.

Luke struggled against the freeze, gasping for air. Before he could open his eyes a strong hand lifted him up by the back of his shirt. He landed on a flat plank, dripping wet, his waterlogged backpack weighing him down. There, next to him, Katie and Tommy shivered from the cold. In the next moment a large net dumped Billy, Lynn, Uncle

Brian, Aunt Eileen, Mom and Dad onto the deck next to them. Several men surrounded them, moving in and throwing blankets over their heads and bodies.

No one was sure how they survived. Nothing made any sense at all until Uncle Al came down from the boom to check on them. "Is everyone okay?"

Still shivering from the cold, Luke, Tommy and Katie all surrounded him in one big wet hug. Uncle Al broke from their embrace when he noticed that Dad wasn't moving. He rushed to Dad's side, "What happened?"

"Janine's goons shot him," Mom said through tears.

"Why?" Uncle Al screamed.

"She thought Holger Danske would save him," Luke explained.

Uncle Al rolled his eyes and said to himself, "He's not a Dane. She should have known that."

"We need to get him to a hospital," Uncle Brian said.

"You're right." Uncle Al turned to the boat captain and instructed him to return to shore. He also had him radio ahead so an ambulance and taxi could be waiting for them. The boat turned and headed for shore.

"So how did you guys get us out of there?" Uncle Brian asked.

"We didn't," Uncle Al replied. "You guys just landed in the water next to our boat."

Everyone was stunned by this uncanny circumstance. Then Mom asked, "Why are you in this boat, right here, right now?"

"I'm not sure," Uncle Al replied, "something just told me this is where I needed to be. This is the spot where Soren's artifacts were found. I figured they had something to do with Holger Danske's vault and how Hans escaped." After a pause Uncle Al asked, "So no one knows how you got out of there?"

Everyone was silent until Tommy said, "It was Holger Danske; he saved us." Tommy then explained how he saw the blinding light whirl above their heads and then smash through the water and the floor below. "We were doomed," Tommy insisted, "and he saved us."

No one wanted to argue. They were out of the vault and all that mattered was getting Dad to the hospital.

When the boat pulled into the dock the ambulance was there to take Dad, Mom and Aunt Eileen to the hospital. Uncle Brian gathered Billy, Lynn and Katie with him and headed for the taxi. He motioned for Luke and Tommy to join them.

"You go ahead," Luke said to Tommy and Uncle Brian. "I'm going to wait for Uncle Al; we'll meet you at the hospital."

Tommy was reluctant to leave his brother, but he desperately wanted to know that Dad was alright. "I'll see you there; don't take long."

"We won't," Luke responded. He hoisted the heavy backpack over his shoulder and labored toward the boat and Uncle Al.

The ambulance raced off with the taxi right behind. Luke waited for Uncle Al as he paid the boat captain for his services. "I'm glad you waited for me," he said to Luke, "I was afraid I was going to have to go all by my lonesome." Together they walked off the pier and onto the nearby street.

Luke shrugged as they walked. "There's something I want to talk to you about."

"I bet there is," Uncle Al sighed. "You've been through a lot over the past couple of months and you probably think I have a lot of answers for you."

"No," Luke interrupted. He kept walking but it took a while for the right words to come to him. "I know you don't have all the answers, but I think you can help me with something."

"What's that?" Uncle Al asked.

They reached the main road, but there was no one about. Luke looked all around to make sure they weren't being watched. "This." He held up his backpack and opened it for Uncle Al to look inside.

"What is it?"

"Go ahead," Luke said, "reach in."

Uncle Al reached into the pack and then leaned his head in for a closer look. "Is this what I think it is?"

"I think so," Luke said.

"So what are you going to do with it?"

"I don't know. I thought you could help."

Uncle Al got a big smile. "Why don't you let me take it?"

Reluctantly, Luke handed over the backpack and Uncle Al threw it over his shoulder.

They continued walking for another couple of miles. Nothing was said; both of them were consumed with thoughts of Dad. When they arrived at the hospital Uncle Al turned to Luke and said, "I'm not big on hospitals." Patting the backpack softly he added, "Besides, I have some things I have to take care of. I'll come back as soon as I can."

"Aren't you going to come inside?" Luke asked, "to see if my Dad is okay?"

"He's in good hands," Uncle Al replied. "Your Dad's been shot and there's going to be a lot of questions. Questions I can't answer without getting in serious trouble. The Danish police and I have a bit of a history. I hope you understand."

Luke nodded as if he understood, but he didn't.

"I'll be back, I promise."

"That's what I thought," Luke said as he watched Uncle Al leave, unsure if or when he would see his uncle again.

31. Wrapping Things Up

It was six days before the doctors would confirm that Dad was well enough to travel. "The bullet missed your vital organs," the doctor explained, "but it caused multiple infections. You're okay to travel, but you should take it easy for the next couple of weeks."

Uncle Brian joked, "Just like you to spend vacation days when it could have been sick time."

Dad laughed until he realized that Luke and Tommy were watching, at which point he scolded Uncle Brian, "That's not funny; don't be a bad influence on your nephews."

In the corner, Mom sat with her arm in a sling, Aunt Eileen was next to her in a wheelchair, her ankle in a cast.

"You two need to take it easy as well," the doctor directed. Patting Luke and Katie on the shoulders he added, "Let these youngsters take care of things for a while."

"I could get used to that," Aunt Eileen said with a smile.

Uncle Brian interrupted in a panic, "Where are Billy and Lynn?" He bolted out into the hall and returned a few moments later with a squirming child under each arm.

Uncle Al followed them into the room. "So how's everyone doing this morning?"

"Uncle Al!" Luke and Tommy shouted, launching themselves across the room to give him a hug.

Uncle Al gave the boys a hug then bent down to give Mom a kiss on the cheek. Crossing to Dad he asked, "So how are you making out old man?"

"The doctor says I can finally travel home," Dad answered with a grin, then added, "Any chance you can come back to the states with us?"

Everyone looked on in anticipation.

"I wish I could," Uncle Al said, "but I have things I gotta do."

"Another adventure?" Luke chipped in.

Several groans escaped from people around the room. "I think we've had enough excitement for a while."

"I do have good news," Uncle Al offered. "According to my sources, Janine and her crew left the country; they were headed for France. As far as I know she still believes that all of you are still trapped in the tomb."

Everyone agreed that they were safest as long as Janine still believed this. Mom was concerned, but Uncle Al assured her that they were all safe now. Despite his confidence, neither Mom nor Aunt Eileen would let the kids out of their sight unless Uncle Al or Uncle Brian was with them.

Over the past week Luke, Tommy and Katie had taken every opportunity to explore the culture and life of Denmark with Uncle Al. They had lots of free time and they made the most of it, taking long walks through old neighborhoods, shopping in neat boutiques and eating in a different café for every meal.

With the news that they were going to be heading home, they were both excited and depressed. When they first got to the hospital and Dad's condition was touch and go; they wanted nothing more than to get back to a normal life. But once they had the freedom of no homework, no parental supervision, no one putting their life in mortal peril, and spending time with Uncle Al, they learned to enjoy the tourist lifestyle.

Uncle Al said his goodbyes to everyone at the hospital. It was sad to see him go but he assured them that he would write more often and that he would not let so much time pass between visits.

"So where are you headed?" Luke asked.

Uncle Al mumbled a response about cold winters in Moscow. Luke let the words seep in. "Wait," he asked, "isn't that where you found Soren Jacobsen's globe?"

A sly grin came across Uncle Al's face but he didn't answer the question. Before he departed he left them with some very special words, "Life's an adventure, make sure you enjoy the journey."

Traveling with a man recovering from a bullet wound has its advantages. On the trip home, they were pushed to the front of every line. When Uncle Brian went to check them in at the airport he got all of the adults bumped up to first class. And when he explained about Billy and Lynn being too young to travel alone, they got bumped up as well. Luke, Tommy and Katie were left in coach, but they didn't mind.

The flight back went by like a flash, or more like a long nap. After everything that had happened, everyone spent most of the trip deep in sleep. When they got off the plane and made it to baggage claim, a limo driver was waiting for them.

"Janine must have forgotten to cancel the last part of the travel package," Dad said. "I wonder how long it will take her to figure out that we made it out alive."

Everyone pondered the question as they loaded their bags into the limo.

The driver went to Uncle Brian and Aunt Eileen's first, dropping them off with the girls. Even though they had plans to get together the following day, the goodbyes were long and emotional.

When the limo finally dropped Mom, Dad, Luke, Tommy and Billy off at home, they couldn't wait to get inside and put this trip behind them. Dad climbed the front steps gingerly, went inside and collapsed on the living room couch. He put his feet up on the coffee table. He looked like he could stay there for the rest of time.

Normally Mom would complain about dirty shoes on top of her nice furniture but not this time. Instead, she carried Billy in her good arm and took him up to bed. Luke and Tommy carried the luggage in from the limo.

It went unnoticed at first, but on the dining room table was a box wrapped in plain brown paper with string tied tightly around it and stamps from some strange country plastered all over the top. No one said a word as Luke picked up the box, put it under his arm and carried it up to his room.

He placed the box on his desk and took a pair of scissors from the drawer. With a snip of the string and then a couple of precision slices with the blade, he revealed a plain wooden box. He opened the lid and pulled out a pair of nunchuks, Tommy's nunchuks from the pawn shop in Copenhagen. Luke placed them under Tommy's pillow. Returning to the box, he removed the only other item, a heavy object wrapped in cloth. He placed it on his bed, unwrapped the material and gazed upon the beautiful handle of a sword. It had a wire bound grip, long and sturdy with a hexagonal pommel on top. On the other end there was a triangular shaped cross guard leading out to curled edges. It was the most incredible handle Luke had ever seen but it was just the hilt.

Luke picked it up and much to his surprise a solid blade emerged from the base. The blade was four times as long as the handle and the hardened steel glistened and glimmered in the light. He set it down and the blade disappeared. Several times he picked it up and put it down watching the blade appear and disappear before his eyes. Luke inspected it closely, but could not figure out how it worked. He held it up to the light and stared in awe at a weapon of the finest craftsmanship.

Luke wrapped the hilt back in the cloth. Grabbing a flashlight from the desk, he got down to the floor and scurried beneath his bed. Where the floor met the wall he pulled out two pins from the baseboard revealing a hiding place with a safe bolted in between the wall studs. Delicately he turned the dial and opened the door. He removed the sword from the cloth for one more look. When he gripped the hilt, the blade appeared once more. Luke marveled at how good it felt in his hand. He took one more look and noticed an inscription he had not seen before, *"My name is Curtana, of the same steel and temper as Joyeuse and Durendal."* Luke read the inscription multiple times, committing it to memory. He put down the sword and the blade disappeared once again. He wrapped the handle in the cloth and then placed it into the safe.

Who are Joyeuse and Durendal? Thoughts raced through his head as he closed the door and spun the lock. His next adventure was beginning to unfold.

You Too Can Join the Adventure

Like us on Facebook

- **Read a Preview of the Next Book in the Series "The Journey to Joyeuse"**
- **Check Out Additional Stories**
- **Learn Behind The Scenes Secrets**
- **See Images of Your Favorite Characters**
- **And more…**

www.facebook.com/TheStolenAdventure

Check out all the books in The Stolen Adventure Series:

- The Stolen Adventure
- The Quest for Curtana
- The Journey to Joyeuse

Made in the USA
Lexington, KY
16 March 2013